SALTWICK RIVER ORPHAN

HISTORICAL VICTORIAN SAGA

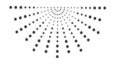

DOLLY PRICE

© 2019 PUREREAD LTD

PUREREAD.COM

CONTENTS

CHAPTER ONE

1863

A pale sun streamed into the breakfast room at Bullmere on this March day. Mr. Westingham ate heartily of his ham, kidneys and toast and slurped a cup of coffee, while his wife picked at her scrambled egg.

The door opened, and Russell entered with a silver tray.

"One letter for you, Madam," he intoned.

"Thank you, Russell," she said, her voice clipped. "It's from Ellen again."

Her husband looked at her in derision but waited until Russell had glided from the room.

"Not from one of your lovers, then?"

She showed him the woman's hand on the envelope, not a fine hand, but undoubtedly female, with *Bullmere* spelled *Bullmeer*.

"What tale of woe has Ellen got for you now?"

"I shall read it later. I want to enjoy breakfast."

"If she's looking for more money, tell her we can't manage it. Yes, I know Oswald's on short time. We've done our bit for him. A job as foreman in my Leeds mill, a position many men would leap at, which he declined." Mr. Westingham spoke in a hurry, with his mouth full, pointing his fork at his wife.

"The selfish man won't leave London! Not even with a family to feed." Jane swallowed a cup of coffee, and ate a little. It would look odd if she ate nothing at all, but she had no appetite. She looked at the man she'd married six years ago. He was uncouth but very wealthy from a wise investment twenty years ago in the railways, which he had poured into purchasing textile mills in the North. Their home was dark grey stone, the largest on Barrington Street, in neogothic style with turrets and battlements, a high and narrow front door and row upon row of pointed windows in the front, thirty in all. Mr. Westingham had intended his house to look great; instead it looked overpowering. The neighbours called it Frankenstein Hall. The architects did not advertise it as their work.

The interior was stuffed to the brim with garish art, curiousities and ornaments, and they entertained lavishly, with no opportunity spared to show their wealth.

Jane, the daughter of a grocer, congratulated herself almost daily on her rise. It had not been easy. She had no wish to be reminded of how her circumstances had almost deprived her of this when it had been within her grasp. Unfortunately, the existence of the child would always threaten her. She already guessed the contents of the letter before she opened it in the privacy of her morning room a little later.

Dear Jane

I have not heard from you. Like I told you we can't keep Gwen any longer. We will have to turn off the nursemaid and will be left with only the maid of all work. We are facing hard times and you have to do your duty and take Gwen now. We were only supposed to have her for three years, and now she's six. I did you a big favour and kept your secret, and you were free to do as you pleased, and *you did very well for yourself. I will expect you on Wednesday. You have to come and take her, <u>or I will bring her to your house.</u> Your sister, Ellen.*

Jane was furious. Gwen had been Ellen's darling until her twins had arrived a year ago. She did not want to write back to her just now—she needed to clear her head, and besides it was urgent to answer Lady Wilder's invitation to her dinner party. She'd worked for two years solid to be invited to this prestigious annual event! But her thoughts would not allow her to put pen to paper. She had to think of a way out of this predicament. She threw the letter into the fire and summoned Martha to get her hat and cloak; she was going to take a walk in the shrubbery.

CHAPTER TWO

The year had been 1855, and Jane Compton, eighteen years old, was living above her father's shop in Highgate. Jane had nothing to do with her father's business, except to spend a great deal of money, which was a matter of continual complaint at the dinner table. Her father's frugality exasperated the socially conscious young woman. He denied her expensive cloth and fine hats, telling her to find cheaper shops. But Jane knew that without quality gowns and millinery, she could not approach near the standard that she wished for herself. Her mother's pleas on her behalf fell on deaf ears.

"You've spoiled that girl," her father would retort. "You've given her ideas above her station, and she'll never be content."

"Mr. Compton, can you not see, that with her beauty, she cannot go about dowdy and ill-dressed? She has something uncommon, has our Jane! I wouldn't be surprised if she married an Earl!"

"You're off your head, Mrs. Compton. I hope no man, Earl or no, will be so foolish as to marry Jane until she has learned to consider the needs of others!"

At this, Jane would cry, push her food away and leave the table in a great huff.

"You are cruel indeed, husband."

Mrs. Compton adored her beautiful, youngest daughter. She was everything she was not, and she was very proud of herself for producing such an exquisite creature, with golden hair, wide cornflower-blue eyes, perfectly formed features and a clear complexion. Her wilfulness showed only spirit. Why should she not do well for herself?

Mrs. Compton had one well-to-do great-aunt, Mrs. Fleetwood, in Grosvenor Square, and by visiting her often and pretending concern for the old woman, she was admitted to her circle of friends. By bringing her beautiful daughter with her, she received invitations to afternoon teas where they mingled with a much better society than they were used to.

Sometimes, out of duty, they went to see Ellen, four years older than her sister, who had married Oswald Peake, the foreman in a foundry near the East End. Mrs. Compton and Jane had been against the match, although Mr. Compton liked the young man.

"You will do much better than Ellen." her mother said to her one day, after another visit to Ellen's modest terraced house in Eastgate Row, near the East India Docks.

"You can be certain of that, Mother." Jane picked her way over some litter on the street, glaring at a ragged urchin who came before them and held out his hand. "This place is full of criminals, look how young that fellow is!"

"Indeed," sniffed her mother, "playing on people's sympathy."

"Get out of my way, ruffian, or I will call the constable, and you will be put in prison." Jane snapped at the boy, who ran away in terror.

At afternoon tea one day at Grosvenor Square Mrs. Compton and Jane were introduced to Mrs. Brown, a talkative widow, who claimed that the cousin of a cousin was somehow related to the Comptons. Jane's mother moved away to speak with another guest, and Jane was stuck in a corner with this Mrs. Brown, who was regaling her with the names and relationships of long-dead relatives. She thought her tiresome and a dreadful bore. She was impatient to get away and speak to Miss Kendall, who was sporting the latest fashion in sleeves, showing them off to two other young ladies.

The drawing room door opened, and the butler showed in a fine, handsome young man, with a smiling countenance and pleasant air. Mrs. Brown looked up immediately.

"Ah, this is Jack at last!" said Mrs. Brown. "My son. Jack! Over here, dear!"

Jane changed her mind about moving away as the gentleman made his way over to them. His fair hair was parted on the side and an errant lock flopped onto his forehead. He had rather unusual eyes, in that she could not make up her mind immediately whether they were blue or green. They seemed blue from a distance, but when he drew closer, they were more a light, clear green. She found them arresting.

His mother introduced them, and Mr. Brown did

not leave Jane's side for the next hour and had asked for permission to call upon her at home before the afternoon was over. Jane granted it, though a bit reluctantly, unwilling to bring him to their apartments above the shop, although they were modern and as stylish as Mrs. Compton could make them. He called, seemed very pleased with his visit, and not at all dismayed by the modest apartment in which she lived, or by her father's appearing in in his work clothes to take a view of his daughter's suitor.

Jane was very deflated to find out that Mr. Brown had neither a good position in society nor a fortune. He was private tutor to a family of young boys. It was not a promising occupation, Jane thought, though she found Jack irresistible, and gave him great encouragement. She told her mother to make herself scarce one afternoon when Jack was to call. Mrs. Compton understood that Jane expected Jack to propose and complied. After her mother had left, Jane sent the servant out on an errand that would ensure her absence for at least an hour. The servant was suspicious, but nobody dared to cross Miss Jane.

Jane's intention was seduction. Jack had high principles and was very surprised, but faced with the clear intentions of the girl he loved with all his heart, they lay together. They would be married, he thought, and he was the happiest man in the world. But to his great shock, Jane turned him down and told him he had better leave before Molly came back —and he was not to return. She dismissed him. He protested—what was her objection? A man was entitled to know why he was rejected!

"Your prospects are poor, Jack. And—there's something in your nature that I find irritating. A lack of spirit. We could not be happy. Here is your coat."

"You do not feel anything for me, Jane?" he said, his throat catching. "I say, I thought you did! I was sure you loved me! Why else—?"

"I don't love you, Jack. I never even think of you when you're not here. Your hat. Go out by the servant's entrance at the back."

He left in confusion at her callousness. He arrived home some time later, got through his dinner with his mother, brother and sister, and made normal conversation. But Robert, older than he was by ten years and his confidant in everything, cornered him later after the women had gone upstairs.

"You have said nothing, Jack. How is it between you and Miss Compton? Perhaps you did not get the opportunity to speak with her alone."

He broke down and told his brother, who had taken the place of a father to him for many years, everything, with sorrow and bitterness.

"I have often heard of a type of man who pretends to be in love with a woman, to use her and then abandon her—but never the other way around. I think, Robert, that I have been used. Have I? What a fool I am. Do you think she meant it, when she told me never to return?"

"Stay well away from her." was his brother's advice. He was concerned though, that an accusation would be brought against his brother by this selfish, wily young woman, and he urged him to leave London for a time. Jack resigned his position, saw an advertisement in the newspaper for a tutor required in Cornwall and left immediately.

CHAPTER THREE

J ane forgot about Mr. Brown as soon as he had turned the corner of the street. When her mother came back, she merely mentioned that she had received a proposal and refused him. Her mother was astonished and tried to get her to reconsider.

"He's a good, steady man," she scolded in her mild way. "You must mean to refuse him so as to make him keener. He's besotted with you and he'll be back."

"Mother, I told Mr. Brown never to return. I don't want to marry him at all. He's only a tutor! He will never be rich! I can do a great deal better. And—I don't want to be a *Mrs. John Brown.*"

"Well here's a turn of events! What's wrong with being Mrs. John Brown?"

"John—or Jack, even worse—and Jane Brown. Mother, how common! I might as well be the wife of a coalman. There must be hundreds of maids in London named *Jane Brown.* I wonder why they didn't make their family name a double-barrel. His mother's maiden name is Montgomery—how did she bear to go from being a Montgomery to a Brown? Now, *Montgomery-Brown* would be very grand. But no, Mother, depend upon this, I will never become a Mrs. Brown."

Her mother accepted her reasoning. Jane was far more knowledgeable in the ways of the world than she was. Jane's father, who was told of it later, was full of contempt for her shallowness. He opined that Mr. Brown had had a narrow escape. That stung, but she held her head high. Besides, she had made Daniel's acquaintance the week before, and soon she would move from above this shop to his new mansion in Chelsea and be mistress of it.

Daniel Westingham. A businessman fifteen years her senior, she'd seen his mansion and was determined to be its mistress. Everything Mr. Westingham touched turned to gold, causing her to overlook his bulldog build, disagreeable, broad features, double chin and bulging eyes that put her in mind of a fish. He had investments in the West and East Indies, in tea, in cotton, in sugar, in everything prosperous. He also had two textile mills, one in Manchester, and one in Leeds, and was opening another in Warrington. He had his hand in shipping. Money was rolling in while he ate, slept and courted Miss Compton.

Her father disliked him, mostly because a large part of his mill workforce was made up of children. Jane was unmoved. If it was legal, there must be nothing wrong with it. She sympathised with Daniel that the Government mandated that the children spend some hours in school, learning. Yes, Daniel was her man, even though she was not at all taken with his appearance. She would be Mrs. Westingham, and escape her father's shop forever.

Then she found out that she was *in the family way*. This was disastrous! She and Mr. Westingham had behaved very properly, and there was no way that she could pass the child off as his. Not for one moment did Jane entertain the possibility of trying to contact Jack Brown, who would marry her in a heartbeat. She confided in her mother and Ellen, forbidding them to tell her father, or to contact Jack. Her mother found out that Jack was no longer in

London. Mrs. Brown said he had gone to Cornwall for the sea air.

Jane met Mr. Westingham, and with a very sorry air told him that she had been summoned to tend a sick aunt in Sussex and would be gone some months. He was very upset, and wanted to accompany her there, and visit her there, but to each suggestion she deftly found an excuse. They parted, promising to write.

Jane then moved into her sister's modest house in the East End, where she demanded the best bedroom, citing the better air there for her health and condition, driving Ellen and her husband to the smaller room at the back. Every week, she wrote to Mr. Westingham, and Ellen faithfully sent her servant to Sussex on the train to post it.

In Highgate, Mrs. Compton was unable to keep the secret. Her husband was furious. He demanded to know who the father was, so he could go and make him marry his daughter. Here, Mrs. Compton lied, and said that it was Mr. Westingham, but that the time was not good for them to marry because of his setting up his new factory, but that they would certainly marry later. The situation had such an effect on Mr. Compton that he suffered a stroke and was unable to speak. The shop closed and Mrs. Compton devoted her time to nursing him.

CHAPTER FOUR

J ane gave birth to a little girl in November 1856 as bonfires blazed outside and effigies of the Guy were carried around the streets.

"Oh, she's a little sweetheart!" cooed Ellen, cradling the infant in a warm blanket. "Look at 'er downy fair hair and 'er little fists! What're you going to call 'er?"

"You choose the name, Ellen. You've been so good to me, I'd like to allow you that."

Ellen was gratified and chose Gwendoline Mary. Her husband was cross.

"Jane isn't interested in the child." he said. "She's giving you a message that you're her mother."

"Oh, no, Ossie. We're only keeping her until she's three, then Jane will take her, or send her to a school for little ones."

But Oswald was right. A few days later, Jane asked, "Will you adopt her, Ellen? You have no children. You may not ever have any of your own, you know."

"Oswald won't 'ear of that. He says if we 'ave daughters in the future, Gwen would have to take precedence over them. You will come and take her when she turns three, won't you?"

Jane promised, but privately thought that Ellen would become so attached to Gwen that there would be no parting.

She returned to Highgate, and to Mr. Westingham's waiting arms, his mansion and his barouche, and they were married three months later. He, of course, had to meet Ellen and Oswald. He was told that Gwendoline was a foster-child, an orphaned Compton cousin, whom Ellen and her husband had taken in. The timing of Jane's absence and the age of the baby might have raised suspicions with a more intelligent man, but Daniel's sharpness did not go beyond how to make as much money as he could from as little investment as possible; he was not given to speculation about this or that, and had no idea anyway how long it took from conception to birth. Daniel's mother, a small thin sharp woman very unlike her son, who Jane loathed on sight, had her suspicions but she dared not voice them.

Jane settled into the life of a wealthy society wife and rarely visited Highgate, although she sent money for a nurse. Her neglect hurt her parents very much. When her father died, her mother asked if she could come and live with her, but Jane regarded her mother as a poor relation and an impediment to her advancing in society.

"I have made the worst mistake in the world," said her mother with bitterness. "Your father was right. I can see now that indulging you made you selfish. May God forgive me! You will never be happy."

"I do not want to hear you speak like that, Mother! I am happy, and I will continue to be so!"

Jane cut her mother out of her life. She only wanted happy people about her, people who told her how wonderful she was. Her mother moved in with Ellen but lost her mind soon after. She had to go to an asylum where she died after some weeks.

Jack's brother Robert wrote to him telling him of the

wedding which he had seen in the paper. Bitterness overcame him for a time, and he vowed to never allow himself to lose his heart again. Sometimes Jane's words returned to sting him. When his charge was sent to boarding school after two years, he was out of a position, and decided to leave England for a time and look for a situation on the Continent.

Jane had not heard any news of Jack since he'd left for Cornwall. He now crossed her mind more than she wished—she found herself comparing Daniel to him in every way, and Daniel was wanting, except in wealth. As for Gwendoline, she rarely saw her and thought of her not at all. She'd never been in her heart, and she'd cut her out of her life. Her third birthday came and went, and to Jane's relief, there had been only a mild question of her being returned. Jane had been sure then that the Peakes intended to keep her. Then Ellen had fallen in the family way and had twin boys. Still, there was no mention of returning Gwen, and Jane had done nothing for her future. It was just as well, because she and Daniel had had a very difficult time around then.

Since her marriage, Jane had had several liaisons, and Daniel found out about one—the Baronet—and threatened to banish her. This unnerved Jane. To be cast off, living modestly in some obscure neighbourhood, and to be shunned by society! It was a one-time foolishness, she said, and she'd been afraid to refuse the Baronet's advances, for she was quite intimidated by his power and prestige.

She had become very attentive to Daniel after that and had been faithful to him. The following year, she had given him a son and heir, Walter Daniel.

If Daniel were to find out about Gwen, he would be eternally suspicious of her. As it was, he had quietly questioned Walter's paternity, but the baby looked so like him, a perfect miniature with short stocky limbs, broad face and prominent eyes, that even his own mother told him that there could not be any doubt. Her duty done, Jane was soon back in society, and old Mrs. Westingham had to move in to supervise the nursery and give young Wally the attention denied to him by his indifferent mother.

Now, remembering Ellen's demand, Jane walked angrily among her tall shrubs and hedges. Her options were few. Not doing anything was out of the question. Ellen would make good on her threat to bring Gwen to Bullmere.

She could, she supposed, place the girl in a boarding school, even take her there herself. But there would be letters to and from Bullmere, correspondence and so on, and there would be suspicions. She'd never be *easy*.

She really wanted her gone. What happened to children who had no families?

CHAPTER FIVE

"But I want to stay 'ere, Aunt Ellen. Have I been bad, that you're sending me away?"

"No, dear, you 'aven't been bad. Your mother wants you to live with 'er now." It was nearly two o'clock, and Aunt Ellen was tying her bonnet under her chin. "There! A big bow, your mother will think you very pretty."

Ellen was a simple woman, steadfast in her affections, and would have liked to have kept Gwen. She consoled herself that she was going to a better life and put out of her mind the kind of person she knew her younger sister to be—a cold-hearted woman. But Ossie had come to the end of his patience. Money was short and Gwen had to go to where she belonged.

There was no doubt in Ellen's mind that Jane had gotten around Daniel Westingham to take Gwendoline into their home. Jane knew how to wind any man around her little finger—except Ossie, who detested her. Daniel must be so grateful for his heir that he agreed to accept the Compton orphan. And now with her nursery all set up, Gwen would be absorbed into the home on Barrington Street without any trouble. She would have a very privileged childhood indeed! The best of everything!

"You'll live in a beautiful big 'ouse, much bigger than this, and have a lovely garden to play in, full of flowers in the summertime, and a pond where you can feed the ducks, and I will come and visit you."

"Will you bring Hector and Charlie to visit me?"

"Of course, I will! I know how fond you are of them. But you have a little brother you know, and his name is Wally."

"Will I be allowed to play with Wally?"

"Of course, you will!"

A sharp knock came to the door, and Ellen flew to open it. Gwen saw her mother standing there. She visited once a year, and she was in awe of her. She was beautiful, her mother! Tall with a white feather in her hat, a white fur muff and a purple cloak that had white fur around it also. She came into the room, a fine lady, and did not sit down.

"I didn't hear your carriage!" cried Ellen.

"I took a hackney and left it a few streets away."

"Why did you do that?"

"No matter why. Come." she said to Gwen, holding out a gloved hand.

"How is Wally?" Ellen asked.

"Walter is in good health."

"Can I play with Wally?"

Her mother made no reply, and Ellen had her first suspicion. But she dismissed it.

"It was good you got around Daniel." she said to her sister.

Jane gave her a fierce look.

"Daniel is not to know of this."

"But Jane—what—where—"

"Don't ask questions! I have found a place for her— that will do."

"Go upstairs and kiss the twins goodbye again," Ellen bid the child, who clambered up the wooden staircase, her boots making little thuds.

"Jane, I have told 'er she's going to live with you."

"You shouldn't have told her any such thing. Ellen, you are a fool. Of course, she isn't going to live with me! I can't have her in the house, do you understand?"

"You're a cruel, heartless mother, that's what you are! What are you planning to do with 'er?"

"It's none of your business. But I have a plan, she will be well taken care of, I assure you."

"She is the best child there is in the world," said Ellen, tearfully. "But Oswald—"

"Oh Oswald, Oswald. You have yet to learn how to manage a man. Well, I have to be going. Call her down now."

Ellen called Gwen to come down, that her mother was waiting. She embraced the child with tears, and a very guilty feeling.

CHAPTER SIX

J ane walked so quickly that little Gwen could barely keep up to her, though she was at a run. The hackney waited some streets away.

"Is it far to your house?" Gwen asked eagerly. Her mother made no reply.

Gwen had never been in a carriage before, and she was sure this was the beginning of a great adventure. She scrambled in and eagerly looked out the window.

After a time, the hackney stopped and Mrs. Westingham told her they were getting out. They walked a short distance alongside a high wall, until they came to a big gate.

A man came out of a small building adjoining the gate and opened it.

"What can I do for you, Madam?" he asked politely of the well-dressed lady he saw there. Was she a patron?

"I wish you to admit her." said Mrs. Westingham, pointing to the girl by her side.

Gwen had been surveying several buildings of red-brick that she could see inside the gate.

"Which one is your house?" she asked. "Where are the flowers?"

Again, her mother made no reply.

"Admit 'er? Why, we can't do that. By the looks of 'er, she ain't destitute."

"Then I wish to see the Master, and hurry about it."

"Very well, Madam. Please come in and be seated, and I will fetch Mr. Dalton for you."

Gwen sat down on a chair beside her mother in the little room belonging to the man. She was beginning to feel puzzled. *Where were they? What did 'admit' mean?*

She felt suddenly afraid and lonely for Aunt Ellen.

She bit her lip, because her mother was looking very angry. Was not this her mother's house, after all?

After a while, another man came and asked her mother to explain what she wanted.

"I want this child admitted. She has no means of support. She's completely alone."

"And what relation are you to this child, Mrs. er—" for her mother had not given the man her name.

"I'm no relation at all. I found her wandering the street."

"You're my mother!" cried Gwen in surprise. The man's face became thunderous.

"Are you her mother?" he asked sternly.

There was no reply. The man looked even more angry.

"This house is for the Destitute," he said. "You look well able to provide for this child. There's no chance at all of our admitting her. Take her away."

"You do not understand," said her mother with great dignity, yet with an icy tone that frightened the girl. "I had her before I was married. She has no home now, and I cannot take her, for my husband does not know of her. You must understand!" Her mother's voice had risen, and now Gwen felt very frightened indeed. What did all that mean, she had her before she was married, and that her husband did not know of her? Such things were beyond her understanding, and she felt a great distress welling up in her.

"Madam, I sympathise with the situation you find yourself in at the present time, but this child is not destitute. You could take her to a school, or to a relative, but I cannot take her here. You have the means to provide for her, and you must. Now if you will excuse me, I have some essential duties to attend to."

At that, they were shown to the gate. They stood outside. Mrs. Westingham stood and stared at her daughter. If the child had known her thoughts, she would have run away there and then.

"Come," she said, holding out her hand. "We must take a journey."

Bewildered, but too frightened to ask questions, Gwen took her hand.

CHAPTER SEVEN

She did not want to be with her mother. It was clear now that she would not go to live with her, and that she'd never play with Wally or feed the ducks in the pond. They had gone on a train, and her mother had ordered her to stop crying, so she held in her tears with effort.

It was getting on for evening, and after they had got off the train, they walked again, away from the station, until they came to a river that flowed beside a road. Soon they came to a town. Her mother went to a shop with little medicine bottles and bought one of them for her headaches. Then they went to where there was a dairy woman with her milk-cow. Her mother ordered a cup of milk for her daughter and took her a little further up the street and seated her on the grass inside a wall, where she took out the medicine bottle and poured the contents into the milk.

"I don't have a headache, Mamma." said Gwen, quite perplexed.

"Drink it, it's good for you." was the order. Gwen obeyed. It had a strange taste.

"I've finished." She gave her mother the cup, who threw it into the bushes.

"Where do we go now, Mamma?" Gwen asked. "Where will we stay tonight? Can I go back to Auntie Ellen?"

"Yes, I will take you back to Ellen. But first, we will go and look at the river. Come on, then." Mother half-pulled, half-dragged her along a pathway that was leading farther away from the road and toward the river. It was very quiet. Gwen began to feel very tired, so tired that her legs would hardly keep walking.

CHAPTER EIGHT

Jane pushed on, pulling the child after her, the child who was now thoroughly reluctant, perhaps even sensing danger, and drowsy at the same time. She'd laced her milk with laudanum.

There was only one course of action open to her and that was to put an end to this nuisance once and for all. She shut her conscience down, for something like it had begun to surface, and disturb her. She reasoned with herself that this child, this nobody, had no right to exist. She was the result of sin and foolishness. There was no place for her in the world. Surely God must agree with her, if there was a God. She had never consulted Him about anything in her life and regarded those who did with contempt. Her life was hers to do what she wanted with. And this child was in danger of ruining her.

"Please can we stop for a minute, Mother? I'm tired!" pleaded Gwen.

"Very well." Gwen curled up on the pathway. Almost instantly, she fell unconscious.

Mrs. Westingham looked about her briefly. The place where they had halted was a bank sloping steeply toward the river. The opposite bank was choked with reeds and rushes and beyond them, tall trees that now had dark shadows. She looked up and down the bank, and then the water, and saw nobody, no boat, no sign at all of life.

The laudanum had taken effect. She bent down to her. Gwen's face was white and still and her hands were limp.

She could abandon her here. But if she woke, she could, at six years old, relate where she lived. She could ask to be taken back to Eastgate Street, back to Ellen. And that would be the end of everything, for Ellen and Oswald would be so angry that they might tell Daniel. No, that must not—could not—happen! She took up the child in her arms and carried her a little way toward a short, rough wooden pier that jutted out into the water.

CHAPTER NINE

"I 'eard a splash there," the fisherman said. He and his friend were in their rowing boat, half hidden by the reeds on the bank.

"I did too," said the other.

"Oh, will you look there; I say, Bert, look up!"

Bert turned his old eyes to peer through the reeds that hid them from the sloping bank.

"Now why would a fine lady be runnin' like that away from the pier?"

"Maybe someone went in, and she's runnin' to get 'elp!"

"No, not at all! She'd scream, wouldn't she? She's

after throwin' something in, that's what, but why run?"

"Maybe a dog, and she's afeard he'll come out and follow 'er."

"I 'ear splashings. Listen. Let's go an' see, Bert."

The men pushed out from the reeds of the bank and rowed toward the pier.

They rowed swiftly, and as they did, they heard faint cries.

The shock of the cold water had woken Gwen. Then she had gone under and had the unbearable sensation of her nose and throat filled with cold water so that she could not breathe. She'd surfaced momentarily, splashed about, gone under, resurfaced, and managed faint cries, and gone under again.

"I saw something—a child!" Bert had glimpsed her before she sank again.

Together the two men rowed to the place, and Andy dived in, resurfacing with the child in his arms. Bert pulled her into the boat, and laid her on the bottom, where he delivered several thumps to her upper back. Gwen came to, vomited a quantity of milk and water, and coughed as if her lungs would burst.

"Poor little mite."

"We got her just in time, I'd say."

"What do we do?"

"It's late now, we'll go home. My missus will look after her for the night. We'll see about what's to be done tomorrow."

They rowed downstream to an island shrouded in fog where they brought the boat up onto the bank, for there was no pier. Andy swung the little girl in his arms and trudged his way along a beach and turned to a path that led him to a group of humble cabins halfway up a hill. Wisps of dark smoke coiled from the chimneys, and the aroma of fish cooking filled the air.

"Nuru! I have someone here for you to look after," he called out, bending his head to enter his doorway, as a woman looked up from laying plates and cups on the table. "Someone tried to drown 'er."

CHAPTER TEN

J ane ran quickly from the pier. Gwen's eyes had suddenly opened as she had gone in, looking straight at her. That and the splash had unnerved her greatly. She halted to take a breath, and seeing some people on the opposite side of the road, contrived to look composed. She walked quietly along. A mist had begun to fall, and she put up her umbrella, grateful that it hid her face.

Had she really done what she had done? It was called *Murder*. She felt suddenly very, very afraid. It was a new feeling for her.

She passed the dairy woman with her cow, who hailed her.

"Where's my cup?" she shouted angrily.

She hailed a hackney to make her way home. She felt tormented.

"What kept you so late?" asked Daniel after she returned. He was impatient to eat dinner.

"I went to see Ellen. I stayed longer than I anticipated."

"Your son has a fever," said her mother-in-law accusingly. "I have sent for the doctor."

Now here was something else to be feared—that Wally would die, a punishment for what she had done. With a sickening feeling, Jane saw her future. She, who had never known fear, would from now on be filled with it. Fear of being punished, for though she proclaimed she did not believe in God, it was not really true. And there was the fear of being found out and accused of murder. Fear of being hanged.

She trembled, said she was not hungry, and escaped upstairs, looked at her feverish son, and wondered why she could not love anybody, not even her own children.

The doctor came and said Wally would recover. She began to relax. There would be no bolt of lightning to strike her down. She could resume her life now. Her peace would return.

CHAPTER ELEVEN

Gwen was barely awake but was conscious of the gentleness of the hands that cared for her and the tenderness of the voice that spoke to her. She was in a kitchen, was held on a woman's lap by the fire and wrapped in a towel. Women gathered about her and there was a great deal of murmured talk. One woman dried her hair, and another rubbed her cold feet with vigour. Then the woman on whose lap she sat, the woman with the white cap and the dark face, pulled a warm nightgown over her head. She was wrapped up in blankets and laid on a little bed next to the fire. She slept deeply, and spent most of the next day in bed, coughing, and the dark woman, whose name was Mrs. Paul, fed her broth and bread and mashed potato. She fell into a deep sleep that night but woke in complete darkness with a nightmare about not being able to breathe. She sat up suddenly, in panic.

Her strangled cry brought Mrs. Paul to her bedside, carrying a candle, which she put on the hearth as she sat to rock the girl in her arms as if she were a baby.

"Tha's orright, luv, you cry as much as you please. You're safe now, nobody can 'urt you 'ere. Are you comfy, luv? That there is my Daphne's bed. She isn't 'ere anymore, my Daphne. She always said it was very comfy. Are you comfy, then?"

"Yes," whispered Gwen. The gentle fingers stroked her forehead. As she woke up a little more, she remembered what had happened and a great shivering went through her.

"There's no need to be frightened, girl. You're safe as houses 'ere. Who was that woman on the riverbank?"

"My mother," whispered Gwen, her eyes wide with shock and not a little fear.

"Yer mother!" the woman was astonished. "Why din't she jump in after you?"

Gwen bit her lip as her eyes filled with tears.

"I don't know."

"How did you end up in the water, luv?"

"I don't know." Gwen was unready to face how it had happened. She had a brief memory of seeing her mother's face above hers before she struck the cold water. Her beautiful mother, the white feather in her hat touching the sky, her eyes cold, cruel. It was too horrid to even think of!

"What's yer name?" The woman hugged her closer and stroked her hair. Aunt Ellen used to do that.

"Gwendoline Compton."

"Well, Gwendoline, you try to sleep again, and look —our hound is there by th' fire, and he'll see you come to no harm. Do you like dogs?"

"Yes."

"Good, cos Rascal there is very fond of children. How he misses Daphne! Try to go to sleep again now, child, and we'll see you in the morning."

"Is she orright?" Andy asked, when his wife rejoined him and blew out her candle.

"Aye, that she is, and that fine lady you saw running away was 'er mother, she says."

"Her mother! No, surely not! God 'elp the poor child!"

"She's over whatever it was she was drugged with. The doctor said that when she got sick in the boat, that it saved 'er life. As it was, if she hadn't drowned, she'd 'ave died from that, whatever it was, maybe opium. That woman is a wicked one. I 'ope poor Gwen can forget all about her now. She is very comfy in Daphne's bed." said Mrs. Paul. There was a tone to her voice that Andy could not miss.

"We'll have to consult the Council, Nuru."

"It's nearly like having my Daffy back again." Nuru's voice was muffled as she settled under the blankets and hugged her pillow.

CHAPTER TWELVE

The island of Saltwick lay almost hidden from the world in a secluded tributary of the Thames near the Estuary, called the Wick. Invisible from ships that sailed the oceans, most sea-captains did not even know it was there. In low tide, it was accessible from the mainland, if one had a mind to wade ankle-deep in mud to a small town named Rush. In winter, it was cut off completely and accessible only by boat.

Saltwick was six miles long and two wide, and had about eighty families who lived by fishing, basket-making and scavenging the mud at low tide. The inhabitants did not much like 'the World,' as they called the mainland, and 'the World' very much looked upon the people of Saltwick as inferior. The island was of no strategic importance in wars, and people had always lived on it, but were thought to be slightly mad, so were avoided as much as possible. During the Napoleonic Wars a press gang came to take the men of the island for the Navy, only to find none there. They were hiding in secret coves and tunnels.

They were a clannish people, and did not welcome strangers, but had acquired the name of harbouring people that were in need of asylum. In the 1750's four Africans escaped a slave ship at the West India Docks and made their way there. The islanders had hidden and fed them. Though they were free on English soil, they feared kidnap on the mainland by agents of the slave traders, and stayed in Saltwick, meaning to return to Africa someday. Instead they took to fishing and vegetable farming and married locals. After that, word spread as far as the London Docklands that if you fled to Saltwick, you would be safe from danger. Over the years several sailors who had been severely punished, and even a ship's captain who was to face court-martial—had deserted and found refuge there. Two servant girls came. Their employer was a judge whose wife had accused them of theft. They were safe on Saltwick. Many inhabitants had stories of how their ancestor had come to the island, and others, like the Marcus family, and the Pauls, had lived there since Roman times.

The people were not certain who owned the island, but whoever he was, he never bothered to visit or collect rents. Their Member of Parliament never came. The people were of different Christian faiths, and there was a small stone church building, and pastors and priests came when invited to marry, bury, and baptise.

Saltwick's first citizen was called 'the King.' They had always had one, and they kept quiet about it whenever they went on the mainland. It was not an inherited title. Saltwick's King, and his Council, were elected by the men of the island every six years. The King was not addressed as *Your Majesty*, had no court, no treasury and did not collect taxes. Nobody bowed to him, nobody paid homage; it was as if they couldn't think of any other title long, long ago when they first chose a man to lead. Or perhaps it had been a nickname, centuries ago, for the first leader of Saltwick, and it stuck.

King and Council met erratically, but if anything unusual occurred, the matter was brought to their attention at the earliest opportunity. A teacher came to begin a school on the island some years before. The

Council saw no necessity for education of that kind. Boys became fishermen and carpenters, and girls became housewives and made baskets from willow. Everybody grew vegetables and kept fowl. The teacher was thanked politely, then put back on his boat and sent away. A young missionary doctor got a better reception. They needed a doctor, for he happened to be there when a man was injured from a fall, and he saved his life. He had settled and married an island girl. As well as doctoring the population, he read any letter that arrived and wrote any that needed to be taken to the post office in Rush. His children were the only ones who learned to read and write.

CHAPTER THIRTEEN

The present King was Mr. Marcus, and Council meetings were held in his abode, a good cottage with a large kitchen. The table was cleared, and chairs and benches put on three sides to seat the seven members of Council. One chair was placed on the fourth side to seat any applicants for justice, for there were squabbles and disputes as with every community.

There was no jail for criminals. A person who committed a crime was simply ordered to leave the island, for a specified time—or forever if the crime was serious. An occasional escaped convict made their way to the island, but these were speedily despatched back to the mainland—the islanders would not have the police coming looking for escaped criminals.

Dr. Gibson came in with his papers and quill pen and bottle of ink. He noted down those present and the Minutes. When he had first come to the island, Mr. Beasley, the King at that time, had had to be won around to note-taking, the doctor explaining to him why they were important. He would read out 'the Minutes' at the end so that all could agree that they were correct, and for that reason, 'Minutes' were important, especially if there was any dispute later. The King grudgingly gave in.

Any islanders who were free from their duties could come in and stand around to hear the proceedings, and since it was an occasion to hear all the news, the room was usually full.

Today, everybody was curious about the child who had come. An adult applying to stay was novelty enough—but they were avid to hear about the little girl. How did a child come to be among them?

First, The Lord's Prayer was said, and then Mr. Marcus announced that Mr. Benjamin Waites, the painter, was expected soon, and would be staying with him. The island was getting used to artists, and Mr. Waites had come several times.

Mr. Andy Paul got up from his seat—for he was a

Council Member—and took the seat of the applicant.

"It concerns a little girl that Albert Foster and I found in the water at Rush Pier," he began. "She's now in the care of my wife. As you know, we lost our daughter last January. The workhouse killed her."

Resources were limited and food in winter scarce, so scarce that sometimes the islanders had to very reluctantly take a boat across to 'the World' and admit themselves to the workhouse for a few months.

There was a murmur of assent and sympathy. Daphne Paul had entered the workhouse healthy—if hungry—and died there.

"My wife wishes to keep this girl, Gwendoline. As for 'er own circumstances, Gwen, as we call her, is the victim of an attempted murder *by 'er own mother*."

There was a horrified gasp followed by an outburst of chatter.

"How do you know that?" Mr. Marcus rapped his polished walking cane on the table leg in an order for silence. Lacking crown or sceptre, his stick had the mark of authority. He had received it from a photographer as a gift for allowing him to take photos of Saltwick Island. Three of those new marvels had been sent to him and were displayed on the wall.

"She told us."

"Children can lie, or imagine all sorts of things. She could be just a runaway who fell in."

"Bert and I saw a woman running away, and it was not to get 'elp, for she was not screaming or crying, as any mother would be if her child fell into the water. It appears that Gwen used to live with 'er aunt, and then 'er mother came to tek her to live with 'er, but instead of that, she was taken to the river and thrown in at Rush Pier."

"An attempted murder!" said Dr. Gibson, looking over his spectacles, his quill in his hand. "Do you not think we should get the police in this case? If the girl can direct them to her aunt, the police will no doubt find her wicked parent. That woman shouldn't be allowed to walk free."

"No police." said Mr. Kwami, a grandson of one of the Africans, and uncle of Nuru Paul. His opinion was heartily endorsed by everybody else. Every islander knew why police were not welcome.

In 1801, three men from Saltwick had been wrongly accused of poaching on the mainland. They had been hanged. It had created a very bitter feeling among the people of Saltwick. They loathed any visit, for any purpose good or bad, from the police. If a suspect in a mainland theft was discovered to have come from Saltwick Island, the visiting constable, readily visible on his approach, found nobody available for interview. Everybody, except for a few old people who all seemed to be deaf as doorposts, went into hiding on the island. The policeman went home after a fruitless day, hungry, hoarse, muddy and defeated—and vowing to hand in his badge if he was ever ordered to come again. The police generally left the people of Saltwick alone.

"Can you afford to keep 'er?" asked the King.

"Course I can," Mr. Paul looked insulted, and a shadow crossed his face as he remembered Daphne.

They voted that the little girl could stay.

CHAPTER FOURTEEN

Gwen sat up in bed and looked about. The room had a table and chairs by the window, and a dresser full of dishes. A white ladder led upstairs to a place under the roof where there were bundles of twigs and stacks of baskets. A door near the ladder led to another room; she supposed that was where the people slept.

The fire was burning brightly, and a black kettle whistled. She smelled something cooking.

She scrambled out of bed. Her nightgown trailed the floor, and the sleeves hung past her hands. She pushed the cuffs up and went to the window and looked out. She saw the sea on one side with boats bobbing up and down. She had been brought here in a boat. Beyond the boats, across the water, was land. Was that the place where she had almost drowned?

She was hungry and forlorn. She sat back on the bed, pushing her long fair hair back behind her ears. Wasn't there anybody about to give her something to eat?

Then she heard voices, and Mrs. Paul appeared in the doorway from outside, bending her head to come in.

"Oh you're up! Look at you, you're lost in that nightgown. It was Daphne's. She was ten. You must be 'ungry, luv. I 'ave porridge for you."

She went to the dresser and took a bowl from it, then to the fire and opened the pot hanging above the flames. Taking a ladle from a hook, she slopped some porridge in. After she had put a spoonful of sugar on it, and milk, she put it on the wooden table and told Gwen to come and eat it. Gwen did not much like the porridge. It tasted burned. But she said nothing, only ate it bravely, and a piece of bread after that, followed by a cup of milk.

"You can call me Aunt Nuru if you like," said Mrs. Paul. "And, you can stay 'ere."

"Today?"

"For as long as you like. Forever, for we think you need a home. You do, don't you?"

"I want to go back to Aunt Ellen." said Gwen, her head down.

"I think you'd best stay 'ere, Gwen, you're safest 'ere."

Gwen considered this while chewing a mouthful of bread. A deep gloom enveloped her. Again, she could not believe that her beautiful mother had been so cruel. Was she a very bad girl, then?

"Don't look so sad, Gwen. You'll be 'appy 'ere, and there are lots of children for you to play with. You won't be lonely."

"What's that up there?" Gwen looked toward the place where the baskets were.

"That's the loft. Did you never see one? We keep all our things up in the loft. Not that we 'ave much. When you're bigger, we can put your bed up there, if you like."

"Can I really sleep in the loft? When I'm big?"

CHAPTER FIFTEEN

J ane Westingham woke up, and the first thought in her mind, again, was that she was a murderess. Her maid brought in her tea, and she drank it down, almost wishing it was something that could blot out the memory of the last couple of days.

"Are the papers in, Martha?"

"Yes, madam."

"Put them all in the morning room for me."

She had remembered something. As she had been walking quickly away from the Pier, she had heard a rustling in the rushes nearby, but had thought it to be a bird. But was it? Had there been somebody lurking there, and had they seen what she had done?

She pored over the newspapers, her heart in her mouth. She felt she was being *watched*. Who was there to watch? *Pull yourself together, Jane!* She turned page after page, and found no report that a child had been drowned in the Estuary. Perhaps she had not been found yet.

She took up her pen to write to her sister, before her sister wrote to her, or worse, turned up on her doorstep demanding news.

Dear Ellen, you will want to know how Gwendoline fared. I brought her to the workhouse, and they took her in, but said that as they were full, and were about to send some other girls to a workhouse in the North, they would send her there also. I do not know where. But she is safe and well and do not worry about her. You have done your duty. I have done mine. Your loving sister, Jane.

The following morning, she examined the newspapers again, but found nothing. She went about that day feeling weighted down by invisible chains, and that annoyed her, because she was meant to feel free. She could not shake them off.

At breakfast the following day, a letter was brought in for her in Ellen's handwriting.

"I think you should know that Ellen's ward has left them." she said casually to her husband, after opening and reading it. "A relative came and took her away, to the North, I believe. It's just as well. She was a burden."

"Well that was rather heartless of them, I should think." said Mrs. Westingham. "She lived all her life with Mrs. Peake, did she not, since infancy? And then a stranger comes and takes her away. How does Mrs. Peake know this relative will treat her well?"

"She was not a stranger, actually. The child—er —*Gwen*—knew her from visits and was quite fond of her. It was always on the cards that she should go to her." Jane felt uncomfortable. She had had to force the name *Gwen* from her lips. She cast her eyes down to her plate.

Mrs. Westingham glanced at her. "You never mentioned it," she said. "I thought that she had nobody at all."

"My sister has not been as forthcoming as I would have liked. Anyway, it is none of *our* business." Jane trembled, losing her composure for almost the first time in her life. This was disconcerting. Her mother-in-law was an astute person, unlike Daniel, and she became afraid that somehow, she knew more than she was supposed to.

But her mother-in-law was silenced at that rebuke.

Later, she burned the letter from Ellen. It had run thus:

Jane, you are a cruel, heartless woman. How can you be so callous to your own child? But you never had any feeling for her. When I told Oswald, he said that if we had known of your plan, we would have found a way to keep her, rather than allow her to become a workhouse child. You have as good as taken her life. Never come here again. I will never disturb you. You are dead to me. Ellen.

The words had hurt her, for she liked to visit her sister now and then. What if Ellen knew what she had really done? But it was all very well for Oswald to be sanctimonious now that Gwen was off his hands!

After a week of searching the newspapers she decided to forget it as best she could. She began to plan her gown for Lady Wilder's dinner. There was a newly returned Governor of a British colony in Africa, and she'd heard he was very handsome and not in love with his wife. She would have a new gown, rose silk, low-necked, with graduated frills in the bodice and the skirt, and a big bow. She'd seen just the thing in a Paris catalogue.

Drinking, dancing, and being in company would shake off the chains.

CHAPTER SIXTEEN

The south side of Saltwick Island was higher than the north, and there the land was pleasant and green. Most of the islanders lived on this part, in a chain of scattered hamlets, in cabins and cottages made of island stone, growing potatoes and a few basic vegetables in small plots. A few grew flowers in quantities enough to take to 'the World' to sell in summer along with baskets and fish.

A rough road ran the length of the island. There was little winter fodder for animals, and no barns, and only a few sheep and goats grazed the hillside. Any carting done was by men. In the past, fuel was mostly wood, but more boats filled with coal were making their way to the island.

A few lone souls lived by the marshy, muddy shoreline, where bullrushes and reeds grew tall. Nearby, the islanders planted the young willows used for basketmaking. The horns from unseen ships leaving for the farthest corners of the Empire or returning from long voyages were reminders that 'the World' was still there, with its noise, busyness and commerce. Most islanders wanted none of it.

Gwen had always lived on a busy street and for the first few days she found the silence strange. But though she missed Aunt Ellen and the twins, she adapted quickly to her new surroundings. She did not like the milk, but Mrs. Paul coaxed her into drinking it and soon she did not notice the taste. As spring advanced, there were many different things outside to look at. She loved flowers, and the hillside looked as if a big tablecloth of purple and orange had been laid upon it. The wild creatures delighted her. Gulls gave long shrill calls from dawn to dusk, herons hidden in the reeds croaked. Within a month, she felt at home, and had made a friend.

"She seems like a happy child even though 'er mother tried to drown 'er." remarked Mrs. White, stirring a tub of clothes with a pole outside her cabin. Gwen was playing with her daughter Betty, and both were ankle-deep in mud from a foray they had made by the shore. Their loud, excited voices could be heard all over the hamlet.

"Oh she's still frightened; she wakes up sometimes, and I 'ave to go to her. But I don't think she knew 'er mother at all well," said Mrs. Paul. She was briskly chopping eels on the flat rock just outside her cabin. "Her Aunt Ellen, she was mother to 'er. I think it's as she doesn't know what a mother's love ought ter be; that's why she isn't all cut up. What breaks my heart is, that I told 'er, only yesterday, that she could call me 'Mamma' if she liked, and she looked at me unhappy a minute and then said 'I like Auntie Nuru.' I nearly wept."

Mrs. White tut-tutted and they were silent for a few moments.

"Those clothes you've put on the child are miles too big," remarked Mrs. White then. "I 'ave a few pinnies that Betty's grown out of."

"They were all Daphne's. I've been making some of them over. Halloo! Girls! Where are you going now?"

"Gwen wants to walk in the mud again. She likes walking in mud!" Betty called out.

"It's squashy!" said Gwen.

"Those two will be good friends," Mrs. White remarked. "Betty! Don't be long! You 'ave to help me hang the clothes!"

CHAPTER SEVENTEEN

Gwen waded in the smooth, pasty mud, enjoying the squashy way it spurted up between her toes. The horror of the day she had nearly drowned had faded only a little, but Betty was a distraction, and had showed her many places on the island, secret coves, an abandoned lighthouse, and birds' nests in the rushes, from which they ran very quickly when the indignant birds chased them. She was a lively companion and the girls had liked each other on sight. They became the best of friends.

"Who was Daphne?" asked Gwen of her friend. She'd seen that Auntie Nuru had a sadness whenever Daphne's name was mentioned.

"She was luvly, was Daphne! But last winter, Andy Paul had an accident, a broken leg, and 'e couldn't fish. They all went to the workhouse in the World, where they'd have food. But she got bad there and died. They're bad places, those workhouses! Were you ever in one?"

"No, were you?"

"No, but I saw one once. It had a high wall, and a man at the gate, and buildings inside, very big buildings! So many windows!"

Was that the place her mother had brought her to, only they would not take her? She'd meant for her to die there! And then she'd taken her to the river.

"Is it for the—the—*destitute?*" she asked.

"Destitute? I don't know what tha' means. It's for 'ungry people."

Gwen was puzzled. She had not been hungry. Maybe destitute was another word for hungry.

"Wha's the matter?" Betty asked, picking up something that shone.

"Nothing." said Gwen. The guilt that she was bad, that somehow she was to blame for her mother trying to be rid of her, surfaced.

"Look, Gwen, what I found!" Betty triumphantly drew a purse from the mud, its clasp gleaming in the sun. "Let's see if there's anything in it!"

There were a few copper coins, sodden, but none the worse for being in the water. Betty grinned with delight.

"Next time I go to the World, I'll buy a ribbon for my hair, if Ma lets me."

"How did the purse get there?" asked Gwen.

"The tide washes 'em in! We find all sorts of things! My brother 'as treasures! But don't tell Ma or Pa, cos they don't know. They'd take them over to the World to sell. Oh look, Gwen! Over there!"

Gwen followed her pointing finger to a man in a straw hat who had a strange tall object he was securing on the beach.

"Who is it? What's he doing?"

"A painter! That's an easel; there, he's setting up!"

Betty suddenly turned and putting her two fingers in her mouth, whistled loudly to several other boys and girls who were foraging a bit farther away. *"Painterrrrr!"* she shouted and pointed. They surged forward en masse at her news.

Betty skipped along the beach toward him, and Gwen followed.

CHAPTER EIGHTEEN

"Oh, the children have found me out, and so soon!" groaned Mr. Waites, as he saw the girls running toward him, with more children in hot pursuit. "I have not been here three hours yet, and here they are! Wild creatures! No school, no discipline, running about where they please! The ways of civilisation are alien to these young feral creatures! But the children are part of Saltwick, and if one doesn't like their attention, one should not come at all."

He greeted them pleasantly, he actually liked children, but had hoped for at least a half-day before they found him.

"Young ladies." he bowed.

Gwen curtsied in return, like she had seen Aunt Ellen do with a grand old lady once who had stopped her carriage outside her house and asked for directions. Betty attempted to copy her, and almost lost her balance.

"We have not had the pleasure of an introduction," Mr. Waites went on. "I am Mr. Benjamin Waites."

"I'm Betty White. You met me last year and you don't remember! And she's Gwen. She's new here."

Mr. Waites bowed a second time, causing another flurry of curtseys, amusing the artist.

"You have grown so much, Miss Betty, I did not know you."

"What are you going to paint, Mr. Waites?" Betty asked with excitement.

"I thought I would paint the headland over there, you see, yonder? With the old lighthouse."

But as he spoke, his eyes lingered on the girl called Gwen. She had an interesting face, heart-shaped, with well-spaced features, and a sprinkling of freckles on her nose. But it was not her features that interested him most. Her mouth smiled, but her eyes were sad. Light green eyes, with bluish tints.

Unusual, and striking. If he were to paint them, he would not be certain what colours to use. Jade perhaps, washed lightly with violet. There were shadows in her face. She had a story. What was it? What dark thoughts lurked behind her eyes? What haunted this little girl?

The children sat around the borders of the sheet he had spread on the sand, watching him take out his paints and mixing colours on the palette, and pestering him with questions. But voices calling to some put paid to their plans to sit and watch him work. Their mothers wanted them home; there was work to be done.

Gwen helped Auntie Nuru bake bread. She told her all about Mr. Waites. As they were sitting down to their dinner later, they were surprised to find a visitor—the artist himself, who had found them out.

"Would you like your likeness done?" asked Auntie Nuru eagerly of her, after Mr. Waites had explained his reason for calling. The artist had to explain to Gwen what that was, and she said she didn't mind, though she was sorry the day after, when she had to sit on the rock outside the door for a long, long time while he drew her. He told her to sit and think.

"About what?"

"About your life. About what you feel in your heart."

What a funny man! But she tried her best, though she sighed often. While she sat outside the mud and stone cabin and the wind blew her hair about, she thought about Aunt Ellen and Mother and the workhouse and how she was nearly drowned and how she had come to Saltwick. She thought and thought for what seemed to her a long, long time, until the sun was rising high in the sky. Then he told her she could go in, and she ran back inside to Auntie Nuru with relief. The following evening, he called in with the painting which he'd had drying overnight.

"But you've only done my head and my shoulders." said Gwen, a little disappointed. Her face in the painting was a great deal larger than it was in real life.

"Ah, but what a good face!" said Mr. Waites. "So clear and soft against the background of the hard, rough grey stones of the stone wall. But look, peeping through a chink in the stones, I have added a posy of tiny blue periwinkle flowers, as if they are looking at you. To soften the rocky background, as if they are telling you that all will be well."

"But there are no flowers in the wall of the house, Mr. Waites."

"But that is artistic license!" he said heartily. She did not know what he meant, and neither did Auntie Nuru, for she shook her head before she said, "Why that's very pretty indeed, but as to buying it, if that was your intention, we can't afford such a painting as big as that. I thought you were doing a small thing."

"Oh, dear Madam, it is not my intention to sell it!" he hastily said. "It is for my portfolio. And I will pay you, Mrs. Paul, or the young Miss, for being my subject."

"I see," said Mrs. Paul, not knowing at all what he meant by portfolio. And he was going to do the paying! Artists were a funny breed orright; he wasn't the first to come to the island, and there was always something odd about them. Like the one who took a great liking to a broken chamber pot he saw lying in the mud. French, he'd said. Maybe even from Paris. Nothing would satisfy him until he had painted that old pot. He even painted the twirling flower decorations and painted them scratched. They had laughed about him for a long time.

Mr. Waites gave Mrs. Paul a half-crown, which she

was delighted with. She put it away for the next time she would go to the World, which was when she had some baskets to sell, and she'd buy Gwen some things she needed.

CHAPTER NINETEEN

That evening, after their supper of fish and bread with strong tea to wash it down, Mr. Waites planned to show his new painting to Mr. and Mrs. Marcus. He was curious about the girl.

He did not want to pry into the affairs of the island, he was privileged in being accepted here to paint the scenery and the inhabitants, for he had seen a few more faces he found 'interesting' and wanted to capture them also. But Gwen was not of the island, of that he was certain.

He had a bottle of whiskey with him and brought it out when Mrs. Marcus was knitting and Mr. Marcus was smoking his pipe by the fire, his cane propped beside the hearth. A wind blew about the cottage. "I thought you might like to drink a little dram with me," he said, and Mrs. Marcus laid aside her knitting, got up and got three tumblers from the dresser. Three! Was she to drink whiskey also? It appeared that she was not to be left out. Mr. Waites poured a measure into each cup before going to his room and retrieving the canvas.

"How do you like the painting?" he asked them, holding it before him.

"I know so little about the art, I couldn't tell you, but it's a good one of the girl orright, I'd know her from it. Wouldn't you, Mrs. Marcus?"

"It's a good likeness, indeed." said his wife, taking a gulp of her whiskey and grimacing. "Oh, this burns, Mr. Waites!"

"You foolish woman, you never drink it like that; go and get some water!" scolded her husband.

"How was I to know that, Mr. Marcus?" she retorted.

When the water was brought in a jug and their tumblers filled with it, Mrs. Marcus took a more tentative sip.

"Aha, that is better," she said. "You'll have to excuse

me not knowing about whiskey, Mr. Waites, I never drank it afore now."

"I am pleased you enjoy it, my dear lady." said the guest, privately wondering if he had begun a bad habit. He had been told that there was a sort of run-down alehouse on the island, in somebody's home, and there were rumours of a still, but it was not likely that the women drank.

"I hope you do not mind if I make an enquiry, Mr. Marcus. Has little Miss Paul lost her parents? She appears to live with her aunt."

"We know little about her. She came to us not long ago." was the reply.

"So she is not from the island at all?"

"No, she was picked up out of the water at Rush Pier." said Mrs. Marcus.

"Out of the water! Good gracious, how did she come to be in the water?"

"Her mother threw her in, that's how. Didn't want her and threw her in." Mrs. Marcus spoke again as she resumed her knitting, her empty tumbler back on the table.

"But that is abominable, Mrs. Marcus! You should tell the police!"

Mr. Marcus realised at this point that the whiskey had loosened up his wife's tongue, and he threw her a reproachful glance. He leaned over to the artist and said:

"No police, if you please, and if you go telling tales in the World, you'll never be welcome here again."

Mr. Waite appeared flustered.

"Mr. Marcus, I would not dream of breaking a confidence. I have nothing to do with the matter and do not wish to be involved. But can it be true?"

"The girl says so, and the men who rescued her observed a woman behaving in a suspicious manner, running away." Marcus said. "She was well-dressed, a fine lady, by all accounts."

"Perhaps there is some other explanation. Why would a mother attempt to do away with her own child?"

"That is something we cannot fathom." said Mrs. Marcus, her needles clacking. "But she's safe here; we'll look after her. She's one of us now. Oh drat, if I haven't dropped stitches. What am I thinking of?" She began to pick at her work.

"You must mention nothing of what you have heard here tonight in the World," said Mr. Marcus, sternly, instinctively putting his hand upon the head of his cane and rocking it back and forth.

"You can rely upon my word." Mr. Waites was quick to reassure him. He paled a little, for he had often been warned on the mainland that the people of Saltwick were not *normal people*. There were stories told about them in the beer houses in Rush and the other villages around. They lived by their own laws. He wondered how the doctor stood it.

"What do ye do with yer paintings?" Mr. Marcus asked him.

"I exhibit them."

"Exhibit? Where?"

"In Art Galleries, where people can come and view them, and buy them, if they like them."

"And paintings of this girl, and of others on the island, people buy those?"

"Yes, I hope they will do so. But it may be many years before I have enough to make a collection."

Mr. Marcus burst out laughing. "I don't know why anybody would buy a painting of a grizzled old fisherman like me." He chortled. "You are going to paint me, aren't you?"

"I'm sure I would love to," Mr. Waites lied. He'd had no intention of taking a portrait of the middle-aged fisherman but realised that gaining his good will to do the other portraits was important. "Shall you sit for me tomorrow?"

Mr. Marcus puffed on his pipe.

"Of course. My good shirt, Missus, for tomorrow." he said to his wife. He pulled himself up on his chair and assumed an air of importance. "But don't tell people who come to see it, that this is a portrait of the King of Saltwick," he warned. "Because *Westminster* wouldn't like it, you know, and might send soldiers to rout us out. This King business is not for outside the island. Do you understand me?"

"I quite understand," said Mr. Waites, instantly resolving to title his portrait *'The King of Saltwick.'* He thought that painting Mr. Marcus was a very good idea after all.

And what a very peculiar tale about the girl with the sad blue-green eyes. It would be an excellent story to tell while he exhibited the painting, though it hardly happened that way, he thought. The people of Saltwick were almost the stuff of myth, and it would hardly surprise the folks on the mainland if the Saltwickers claimed they had rescued a mermaid. What would he title her portrait? He had time enough to think about that.

CHAPTER TWENTY

Summer was happy for Gwen. She roamed everywhere on the island, her heart captured by the delicate flowers and plants, which she gathered and brought home to put into water or to dry in the shelter of the south wall of the cabin. She quickly learned the names of all of them. Uncle Andy promised her little boxes to grow seeds in so that she could have her own little patch to do what she liked with. Aunt Nuru taught her how to preserve the flowers so that they stayed fresh for longer. One day she gave her a basket and told to pick as many good flowers as she could find, with their roots. She filled the basket, and they put the roots in sugar water, and she and Nuru got up very early the next morning. This time they picked the flowers from the garden they cultivated. Nuru got a spool of white ribbon and tied the blooms into bunches and posies.

"Will there be any growing next year, Aunt Nuru, when they don't have their roots?"

"Don't worry, child, the wild ones will be back, for the bees are buzzing. And I 'ave seedlings for the garden ones."

"I feel sad that they are gone from their homes, Auntie Nuru."

"Everything that goes, comes back," Nuru told her, smiling. "And these are meant for our use and benefit. They will make people 'appy, and us as well, because we will have money to buy things we need. Now, put on your boots, Gwennie."

"Auntie Nuru, my boots! They don't fit me anymore!" cried Gwen. She had run about in bare feet since her arrival on the island. Her soles were tough as leather now, but boots were necessary for town.

"Oh, well! They shrank that day in the water! And you're growin' fast too! Wear Daffy's, though they might be too big. We'll pack the toes with straw."

"Come on then, time to go." A little while later Auntie Nuru gave the basket of flowers to Gwen to carry. "Time to cross to the World." Nuru pushed a barrow full of new baskets of all sizes.

It was Gwen's first time off the island since she had arrived there, and she felt a little excitement mixed with trepidation.

"What if my mother is over there?" she said anxiously. She had not mentioned her since her first days on the island in March.

"Don't you worry about 'er. She's not there." promised Mrs. Paul, almost overcome with sadness that a child should regard her own mother with terror. To herself she said: *I'd like to meet this woman, I'd tell 'er that she din't deserve to 'ave a child! Especially such a beautiful and sweet innocent child like Gwen!* She took Gwen's little hand firmly in her rough one.

They were joined by other island women with their baskets to sell, and the children, like Gwen, carried baskets filled with flowers. They walked the two miles across the dried bank and came to a laneway that brought them into a street.

Gwen was conscious of people staring at them as they went up the street. The islanders dispersed to various locations to sell. Auntie Nuru stopped beside a busy corner near an ostlers.

"Willow baskets, cheap! Flowers, luvly flowers, fresh!" she called out to the people passing by. Some people stared at them, ignoring and avoiding them.

Gwen heard *'Saltwickers'* whispered. And then: *'Look how old-fashioned she's dressed!'* of Auntie Nuru. But their baskets sold briskly, and the flowers went too. Gwen chimed in with Nuru to ask people to buy flowers. She was beginning to enjoy herself. If Nuru espied a pair of lovers arm in arm, she chirped: *'Flowers for yer sweetheart, Mister!'* This raised blushes, and smiles—and sales.

Gwen was becoming hungry. It had been a long time since their early breakfast. Aunt Nuru unwrapped a loaf of bread and a few smoked herrings which they ate with a drink of water from a pump.

When they had sold everything, it was time to buy. Auntie Nuru led her up some streets and Gwen realised that they were the same streets that she had taken with her mother. But what a different feeling she had then!

"Would you like a cup of milk, Gwennie?" asked Nuru. She had taken to calling her Gwennie of late and Gwen thought it was nice.

They were in front of the same dairy-woman with

the milk-cow, and Gwen stared at her, so that the woman stared back. Recognition came into her eyes.

"Hey-day! I know you!"

Nuru looked at the milk-woman curiously and drew Gwen closer to her side.

"This is my daughter." she said. The dairy woman raised an eyebrow quizzically. The woman and child did not at all look like mother and daughter, one dark-skinned and the other pale. There was a mystery here, and she decided to try to find out more.

"Beg your pardon, then. I thought it was a girl I gave a cup of milk to, who I remember, because the cup never came back, and the woman—quite a lady too —passed by without the child a while later. The cups being sixpence each to buy, I went looking for it, and found it over there behind that wall, and to make a long story short—there was white powder on the bottom, and I thought, *Something's up.* and I wondered—you see, I was afeard it was something bad!"

As Nuru began to hurry Gwen away, the woman called: "If anything had happened the child, they'd 'ave said it was the milk 'as harmed 'er, and my little milch cow is as clean and healthy as you'd find!"

Gwen was very shaken after this, it was so direct a reminder of that terrible day that a cloud came over her, and her happy morning had vanished as a result.

"Ah, here's Andy now," said Nuru, with relief a short time later, as they espied him lounging by a wall.

"How did you get here, Uncle?" exclaimed Gwen, distracted from her morose feelings at last. "You didn't walk with us this morning!"

"I comes over in the boat," he grinned. "Shopping now, wife?"

"Gwennie needs new boots. Flour, oatmeal, bacon, soap, worsted to make you new trousers, and a new thimble and black thread. Oh, and a ribbon for Gwennie!"

"What a long list! I see ye've no baskets left, which tells me ye had a good day."

"Little Gwennie charmed 'em all," beamed Nuru. "And the ostlers is a good place."

"Let's buy Gwennie a little treat." Andy went into a shop and came out with a bag of sweets and put them into her hand. Soon her hands and face were sticky with red and green, and walking between them, she felt happy.

They shopped in an Emporium, and the shop boy brought the supplies to the boat in a wheelbarrow. But when Gwen saw where they were going, she hung back. It was the same place that her mother had brought her to that day and it was the very last place on earth she wished to go.

"C'mon luv, you're in no danger." urged Nuru. But the entire memory was playing itself out in her mind, and terrified, she broke away from Nuru and ran, leaving a trail of sweets behind her.

"Gwennie! Gwennie!" cried Nuru, taking after her. She caught up with her and swung her into her arms and started back.

"You'll come to no harm with us, luv. Go on, close your eyes and put your head on my shoulder, and you'll be in the boat afore you know it."

"I'm afraid." said the little girl in a small voice.

"There's no need to be afraid with us, Gwennie." Nuru soothed her, thinking that whoever had caused this child to suffer needed to be in chains. Even the milk-woman had noticed something amiss when the lady had returned without Gwennie! Wait until she told Andy about that tonight!

Gwen sobbed quietly, her head buried in Nuru's

shawl so that she could not see anything. She allowed herself to be carried onto the creaking wooden pier without protest and was handed carefully into Andy's strong, sure hands. There were other islanders there now, all met by boats, all going back to Saltwick with their supplies. Everybody had had a good day; the atmosphere was cheerful, and all people wanted to do was to go home and eat some of the purchased luxuries. Gwen clung to Nuru until they reached the island, then she looked up and her tears dried. She was home and ran up the beach to Rascal, who was bounding to greet them.

Betty met her later, after they had had a good dinner of fried bacon and potatoes. They wore their new ribbons and went for a walk.

"My brothers are in trouble," she giggled. "Johnny and Charlie got these—'peer—peerodicals,' they call them, for the drawings in them. They cost a penny each."

"What kinds of drawings?"

"Oh, murders and such!" chattered Betty. "This man, it shows 'im striking 'is wife. Then it showed 'er dead on the floor. Then it shows 'im being 'anged."

"That's horrid!"

Betty was paying no attention.

"But my brothers—now they're sayin' they want to learn to read. But Ma is saying they're not going to the World again if they're bringing back pictures like that. And if Mr. Marcus sees them, he's going to belt 'em with his stick!" She laughed heartily at the thought of the King laying the stick about her brothers. "Ma put the *peerodicals* in the fire. She calls 'em *Penny Dreadfuls*."

"I was learning my letters in the World," Gwen said, remembering. "ABC." Betty, however, was not a good listener and prattled on about the trouble her brothers were in.

That night as Gwen was falling asleep she wondered if her mother had been caught throwing her into the river, whether that would have been in one of these *peerodicals*. Her thoughts became morbid in the dark, so that she lay awake for quite a while. The following day she told Auntie Nuru all about it as she helped her to bake the bread.

"I might have been in one of those 'orrible *peerocicals*," she said. "I don't like that. People looking at me drownded."

"Well it din't happen so don't worry," Nuru said. "God din't let it 'appen."

"Auntie Nuru?"

"Yes, Gwennie."

"You told me the Commandments. It says *Honour Thy Father and Thy Mother.* I don't know my father, and I don't want to know my mother."

Nuru was silent as she shook more flour into the bowl of sticky dough and began to knead it.

"Gwennie, you have an uncle and an auntie for a father and a mother. Tha's what God arranged for you. It's a bit different to other folks, I know, but—" Nuru's voice trailed, for she did not know what to say next.

"I suppose if I don't have a father and mother to honour, God means me to honour you and Uncle Andy."

Tears blurred Nuru's eyes and she wiped them away with her wrist, for her hands were dripping with wet dough.

"Auntie Nuru! You forgot the salt! Here!" Gwen leaned over and shook a generous pinch into the bowl. Nuru plunged her hands in once again and began to knead in the salt.

"Aunt Nuru, you said God loves everybody. Does God love my mother?"

"Oh, He loves everybody." Nuru found her voice. "But your mother—does He love 'er …?" She hesitated for a moment, her voice trailing.

"She's a lost sheep, Gwennie," she said at last. "She got 'erself lost. He's looking all over for 'er, bad as she is. While the bread is baking, child, I'll tell you a story that Jesus told about a lost sheep."

CHAPTER TWENTY-ONE

1

867

CHELSEA

Mrs. Westingham woke up at eight o'clock. The sunlight streamed in the window and danced on the wall opposite. She wondered if she might be a widow by nightfall. When her maid came in, she feigned sorrow as she hauled herself up on her silk pillows and sighed heavily.

"How was Mr. Westingham during the night?" she asked, settling herself comfortably in expectation of her morning tea.

"Well for sure I don't know, Madam." said Edith with some impertinence.

Jane glowered but said nothing. The servants knew

she cared very little for her husband. He had been ill for some time with stomach trouble on and off, had taken a very bad turn yesterday, and she had to engage a nurse to sit up with him.

At least the interfering old woman was not here! She had not missed her mother-in-law one little bit when she had become ill and had gone to live with her other son, Samuel. She remained in frail health, but still had a sharp mind.

Jane had not sent any message to her or to Samuel that Daniel was dangerously ill. She did not want them about, asking her if she done this and that, questioning her.

After she drank her tea and her maid had dressed her, she went to breakfast downstairs and then to her husband's room. The nurse rose as she entered.

"Madam, I think you should summon the doctor today, he seems worse."

Mrs. Westingham went to the bedside and looked down on the bloated face. Why did it make her heart flutter to think he was dying? *Calm yourself, Jane.* But she could not stop thinking of the money.

"He is no different from yesterday," she said. "No, there is no necessity to bother Dr. Notting. He is very busy with maternity cases around this time. He told me so. You may go and rest," she dismissed the nurse. "If I need you, I will call you."

The nurse was looking at her with something like suspicion, Jane thought.

Four years had passed since Gwen had gone. What was done was done. She was a very wicked woman, she knew. She knew now that she'd made a dreadful mistake. She'd gained nothing except fetters and chains she dragged everywhere with her, invisible to everybody, and the only times she could shake them off was when she distracted herself with men, dancing, wine, and extravagance.

Wally was upstairs in the Nursery. She saw him a few times a week. He thought Nanny was his mother, and that did not disturb her, though Daniel got enraged that she had so little interest in him.

She would send him away to school. She would be free! She would travel on the continent, visiting Paris and Monte Carlo, Vienna and Budapest. Maybe she would go to Cornwall first, for she toyed with the idea of finding Mr. Jack Brown again. She had never met any man quite like him, and if he had by some miracle been successful in life, she would kick herself for not accepting him, though she would be plain Mrs. Brown.

Her husband stirred, his brow covered in sweat. She rose and went to him.

"What is it, Daniel?"

"You—" He said in a strangling sort of way, unable to finish the sentence. Then he smiled, his eyes fixing her strangely.

She did not like the smile, or the look.

"You." He smiled again. "You—unfit mother."

Jane froze by the bedside.

"All in trust for Wally. Samuel—"

She felt faint.

"Unfit mother." He said again, in a sort of spitting way.

Jane hurried to the bell and rang it with violence.

"Get the doctor!" she ordered the maid. "Tell him it's an emergency!"

The dying man smiled again, an odd crooked smile.

"Hurry! Send the carriage for him!" cried Jane. "And

if he is not available, find another! And get the nurse up!"

Her heart hammering in her chest, she walked about, watching Daniel's chest heave up and down with effort. He breathed his last before the doctor came in. His widow's tears were very bitter.

CHAPTER TWENTY-TWO

There was an allowance for her of five hundred pounds per annum. No gentlewoman could live on that pittance! Wally was to inherit everything when he turned twenty-five, and in the meantime, his Uncle Samuel Westingham was to act as Guardian. He would have control over everything! It was a bitter, bitter blow. The house was to be sold and the money realised held for Wally. Her clothes and jewellery she could keep.

Enraged, she prepared to leave the house for a smaller residence. She found a modest home on Grace Street in Chelsea, it was not at all a good situation, between a cobbler and a draper's shop, but at least it was a house, not a miserable flat. She could only afford three servants, two maids and a man, and would only be able to entertain in a very small way. Not that her friends would want to know her now in any case! Imagine having to invite them here! Even her wealthy lovers would desert her! For none of them really loved her at all, and she knew it, at least not enough to pursue her through trouble and poverty.

She could go to court for guardianship of her son, she supposed, but that would eat up her jewellery, and if she lost, she would be destitute. She had to try, though. She could not let that fortune go without a fight.

Her husband was buried and her tears were genuine, not for him, but for herself.

CHAPTER TWENTY-THREE

S ALTWICK ISLAND 1871

"Gwennie? Will you go and look at the potatoes, and see how big they've got, and if we should begin to dig 'em out soon."

"Of course, Auntie Nuru!" Gwen was fourteen now, and fully immersed in island life and knew everything from basket-making to growing the food that would keep them for the winter, when fishing was less. Nuru was deftly weaving a basket, bending the rods to make a lattice pattern.

Their food was running low and they'd have to go over to the World to buy some supplies soon. They'd have to take the boats over, for it had been a very wet summer and the embankment had never appeared.

It was July, and the potatoes should be almost ready to be dug. They'd had some of the new ones, delicious they were, boiled well and flavoured with lard and parsley. The rest were left to grow to their full size, and they would keep very well covered up in the shed for the winter.

Gwen knelt in the garden and dug her shovel into a plant to prise it up.

Odd, she thought to herself. *Yellow and black spots on the leaves, they weren't like that a few days ago.*

She bent and pulled up the entire plant from the earth. She could hardly believe her eyes; lumps of greyish putrefaction hung on the stalks in place of firm, brown potatoes. She pulled up another plant, and another. They were all the same. She threw her shovel against the wall and stood back, wondering if they were all like that. Was the crop ruined?

"What's the matter?" asked Old Man Foster who was passing by and saw her. She held up one of the plants.

"Good Grief, the potatoes! Not the blight!" His eyes bulged with horror. "It happened last time about fifteen years ago. Everybody's crop was rotten!" He set off almost at a run for Mr. Marcus's house, while the neighbours came out of their homes to see what was going on and ran for shovels to dig their own plants.

The news spread like a strong gale whipping the island. Not one potato-grower had been spared by the disease. They remembered that about a week ago, a strange, hot wind had blown up and through the island. Had it been that? Or all the rain?

The blight hit England, Scotland, Wales and Ireland every so often. It was unpredictable and deprived the poor of a staple food. The poorer the people, the more they suffered. The island people had little else to eat in times when they could not fish.

"Will there be no potatoes to eat in winter?" asked Pam Gibson, who was in the Paul house. The children were in and out of each other's houses all the time. "The potato is a comforting food in cold weather, and when you add it to any kind of soup, Mamma says it's as good as a dinner!

Nuru shook her head as she wove the last willow rod through the lattice. She began to turn the ends down evenly to make a smooth rim.

"We'll need bread to eat throughout the winter," she answered. "But flour costs money! And tha's what nobody on this island has. These baskets won't bring in enough to see us through."

Andy came home later after fishing. He handed two perch to Gwen who set them on a board and took a knife to gut and clean them. Nuru related the bad news.

"Hard times ahead this winter." he said flatly.

Gwen was adept at preparing fish, and only a few minutes later it was ready to be fried on the pan. They sat about the table for their simple meal of bread and perch, supplemented by a few carrots and parsnips, for the store of potatoes from last year was gone.

The outer door scraped on the flags as a young boy put his head in the door. "Grandfather says to tell you there's a meeting tomorrow after breakfast."

The room in Marcus's the following morning was crammed. Nobody had gone fishing yet, and the women had left their tubs of laundry.

Mr. Marcus introduced the topic, as if he had any need to. Everybody knew that a lean winter was in store.

"We will not starve." was Andy's contribution, after a

very gloomy prediction was made by Mr. Beasley, the former King, who said he couldn't stomach anything else except a little potato mashed with goats-milk, and had lived on it for ten years now. Andy was trying to be hopeful. "We'll purchase potatoes from the World. Their potatoes aren't affected, Reverend Mason would've told us yesterday, when he came to baptise the two children, if there was a blight over there."

"With what?" asked Mr. White. "There is no money here. Which of us has money?"

"I suppose we'll have to go and work over there, in the World," said Andy quietly. "Any of us men who are strong can go. They're building hotels and such over there, more and more every year. They'll be looking for Hands, won't they?"

"Not in winter, they won't build." grumbled Mr. Beasley.

"There is work over there on the mainland." Andy said firmly. "I intend to go there after the fishing is over, and any man who wants to can come with me."

"What about the withy harvesting?" asked Mrs. Foster. Winter was the season for cutting the willow rods.

"Women and children will manage that," said Mrs. White.

CHAPTER TWENTY-FOUR

The women were sorry to part with their men some weeks later as they left for the mainland. They would stay in cheap, dirty lodging houses, two or three to a bed with vermin-infested mattresses, and have to cook for themselves on the common fire these places had. And then there was the work. Who would employ them? *Saltwickers* often found it hard to get work near the shore. They were seen as unreliable, disappearing to do a day's fishing if the weather was good. They were skilled carpenters though, and those who took a chance on them were never disappointed with the quality of their work.

"If there's no carpentry to be had, I'll get work as an odd-job man, or a navvy on the railroads."

"You don't do that, Andy Paul!" sobbed Nuru, holding him, flicking an imaginary bit of lint from his collar. "You're not young anymore! Navvying is too hard for you!"

"Nuru, Nuru, you're making such a fuss! Stop the crying there. Look, you're making Gwennie cry as well."

"I'll miss you!" Gwen said, throwing herself upon him to embrace him. She never forgot that Andy had taken her out of the water.

"Now, now then, tha's enough." he said, very embarrassed, but pleased.

Gwen had another reason to feel sad. Bob White was going away, and she'd miss him terribly. She thought she might be in love with her next-door neighbour. She'd never really noticed him before the beginning of summer, and one day saw his deep dark eyes as if for the first time and felt her heart flutter. She could not stop thinking about him now, but she kept her new-found love a secret. Bob was eighteen and hardly knew she existed, except to bid her the time of day if they met.

It was nice to have somebody to think about, it passed the long dark evenings after autumn came, when it was just Auntie Nuru and herself, sewing and mending and later bundling the withies together to store up in the warm loft. Rascal, very old now, kept his place by the fire and slept most of the day.

CHAPTER TWENTY-FIVE

The absent men got somebody to write, and the letters were brought over by the doctor. He was rowed to the mainland every week for news and to collect his post. He sent his son around to tell those who had letters to come up to his house and read them out to them. One of the families called was the Pauls.

They sat in the doctor's big warm kitchen while he put on his glasses.

14 Georges Court, Battersea

Dear Nuru, I hope you and Gwen are well. We have moved from Essex nearer to London because there was no work there. Now we've gone our separate ways in various groups. I'm with Billy Foster and John White and we found work doing odd jobs. We stopt in Bromley for a while, then on to Brixton and now Battersea, following the work. We are doing fine. I'm sending over money so you can go to the mainland to get food for Christmas. If we were in Essex we could come home but we can't manage it from here. I'll miss you and Gwennie at Christmas. I have to finish now as Billy and Larry want to write home too. Your loving husband Andy.

"Where again did he say he was first?" asked Nuru, and having got the answer, said, "And where after that? And now? Battersea, where's Battersea? These places sound so odd and strange-like!" The doctor waited patiently while she mused, turning the two pounds over in her hand, which Andy had enclosed. They had to go then, because it was the Whites' turn.

"Papa, why don't the children here learn to read and write?" asked young Gibson, a little crossly later, before he bid his parents goodnight. His father had told him that he would have to help him to write some of the letters back to the men, and he was sure that the chore would be a tiresome one. He had given him a good basic education and he had a smattering of the classics to prepare him for boarding school.

"They don't think it's important, Jim. But it is important, you know that, don't you? The talk on the mainland is that there's more and more of a push toward education. If there's ever a Law, there will be a school begun on this island whether the Council wants it or not. Though you're being raised like a wild goat here, you're going to have a profession. You'll go into medicine like me."

"I may have to move to the mainland then, Papa, to study at Guy's, and perhaps I'll stay there."

His father made no reply except to say, "Go to bed, son."

Mrs. Gibson was trimming the lamps.

"What do you mean, by education? Mr. Marcus will have none of it."

"It will come, Edie. It must. Besides, the King won't be re-elected next time."

"Then who will be—oh no, Dr. Gibson—not you? All those squabbles! The Fosters' running battle with the McDonnells' over the sally tree. Young Harry Beasley claiming that his nets were cut by the White lads, who are a bunch of rascals, we know, but they're not bad boys, and we all know that young Beasley never mends his nets. What a headache you'll have, to listen to all that!"

"There'll be no avoiding it, Edie. I am almost sure of being elected. Almost all of the younger men, and some of the older, want me in. But as to what will happen to this island—truly I don't know. The modern world is coming, they say there's never been an age like ours, with innovations and inventions like trains and machinery. The world is hurtling along and will Saltwick be allowed to stay behind?"

CHAPTER TWENTY-SIX

Gwen and Nuru made their way back to their cabin. Nuru was quiet. She felt that Andy was very far away, farther away than she could imagine. Gwen was wondering about something peculiar that had struck her.

"Auntie, Uncle Andy said he was with Mr. White. But—wouldn't Bob be with them too, if so?"

"Why yes, you're right there! But where had Bob got to, then?"

They did not have long to find out. Mrs. White came in weeping a little while later. Both Nuru and Gwen were alarmed. What could be the matter? Surely Bob had not met with a dreadful accident? They put her sitting down by the fire.

"John had such news for me, I don't know what to say, or do." she sobbed. "Bob is gone from 'im. He and Pat Broome, and Jem Marcus said they wanted to try their own luck and wouldn't stay with their fathers! They've written to nobody at all; who knows what 'as become of them? Why wouldn't they stay with their fathers, who could watch them and keep them from all the evils in the World?"

"They're young men." soothed Nuru after a moment or two. "Young men go a bit wild."

"I met Mary Broome," Mrs. White went on. "Harry wrote that the lads said they were going to—*the North!*" Mrs. White cried into her apron. "*To see the World!* Isn't there world enough for them—over there!" She threw her arm vaguely in the direction of the mainland, hitting her hand off the fire irons, making a clang.

At this, there was consternation. The North might as well be the Moon. It was bad enough to leave the island for any length, but to go to *the North of England!* That was shocking!

"Perhaps he just said it for a jest." Nuru said feebly. "Wait till you see, they'll get sick of travelling and come back. Full of wealth, maybe!" She slapped her friend's shoulder in an affectionate way, and took her hand, inspecting it for a bruise.

A dreadful gloom enveloped Saltwick after that. It was unheard of that someone should go so far away, and that three young men, needed on the island as their fathers got older and less able to provide, would even think of leaving for good (for nearly everyone took the worst from it) seemed to be the most selfish thing in the world. Mr. Marcus looked like thunder, going about the island striking his stick against walls and bushes, and his daughter-in-law could not stop weeping as she sat and knitted socks for the son she was sure she'd never lay eyes on again.

Gwen cried for Bob for two days, together with Betty, who was convinced she'd never see her brother again either. Then Betty began to wonder if her other brothers would want to go also, and that was a fresh thought to cry over.

Gwen's tears dried quickly, and she decided that she must not have been in love after all. Besides, she was to go to the mainland with Auntie soon to buy things for Christmas. Rush Pier held no fears for her now, though sometimes a sadness came over her and she wondered about Aunt Ellen, especially at

Christmas. She remembered a decorated tree in the house. In Saltwick, there were no Christmas trees.

That was all so long ago it seemed like a different life.

CHAPTER TWENTY-SEVEN

The sorrows of the island were softened somewhat by letters from the three errant young men, postmarked 'Leeds.' Bob found work as a carpenter on a large estate. He wrote that his employer was very good, and he had all he wished to eat and drink. The other two were factory hands. None said when they were coming back.

The King sat down with Dr. Gibson to dictate a strongly worded letter to his grandson about ingratitude and duty and an order to return at once, which the doctor silently thought would have the opposite effect to what the King intended. His mother sent him the socks, for he had complained that the weather was cold, with much snow. Mrs. White likewise dictated a letter to young Jim Gibson for her son Bob and said that she hoped somebody would be on hand to read it to him straightaway, for she wished him to know that he was greatly missed.

"Oh, Mrs. White, Bob can read some words. I taught him!"

"You! It's your fault, then! You shouldn't 'ave!"

"But he kept asking me! He wore me out asking! Now did you want to say '*I miss you*' or '*We miss you*'?"

Gwen was interested to hear that the young men had been taking secret lessons from the doctor's son. The Gibsons were different from the other people.

Most of the men wrote every month, and there was feverish excitement whenever the doctor returned from his weekly foray to the World. He humourously suggested to the King that Her Majesty Queen Victoria should establish a mailboat, but this was too much progress for his liking.

Spring came, and the doctor returned from his trip to the mainland one sunny February Friday bringing the post. To Mrs. Paul's distress, there was no letter for her, but when Dr. Gibson entered the cabin about an hour later, accompanied by Mrs. White, both Nuru and Gwen looked up eagerly.

"Oh, is there a letter for us after all?" cried Nuru, jumping up. "You din't have to come down with it, I would've come up ..." her voice trailed away, for Mrs. White had not lifted her head in greeting, and everything in the doctor's countenance predicted ill tidings.

He made her sit down. Gwen stood behind her, her heart fluttering with anxiety. The doctor cleared his throat.

I'm afraid I bear very bad tidings about Mr. Andy Paul. He was working on a building site, and there was an explosion. He was too near it. There were four men killed. Please tell Mrs. Paul that he did not suffer. We gave him a good funeral and clubbed together to buy him a coffin and a grave, so he is buried decent. All the men attended and the foreman. He is buried in the churchyard at St. Mary's.

Utter heartbreak attended this news. That night, and for days afterwards, neighbours looked after the bereaved family as best they could. Both were stricken with shock and a grief that lasted weeks. To compound their sorrow, all of the other men, minus the three truants, returned to the island in March, to jubilation, bringing necessities and gifts. A dance was planned in the King's house. A part of Gwen longed to go, but she bit her lip. They were in deep mourning.

The two men who had been with Mr. Paul had brought supplies for the bereaved family, and the sum of ten pounds compensation from the building company.

"Nothing will ever be the same," said Auntie Nuru, starkly.

CHAPTER TWENTY-EIGHT

CHELSEA

Most of Mrs. Westingham's jewellery had been sold by now. The guardianship case was very expensive, even though the lawyer taking it for her was a little under her spell and was not charging her as much as he charged his other clients. Unfortunately, the case was throwing up some very distasteful revelations. She had been spied upon during her marriage!

Mr. Samuel Westingham was her main opponent, urged on of course by their mother. She'd ignored her brother and sister-in-law throughout most of her marriage. She had nothing in common with Stella, who was devoted to Samuel and spent most of her life attending to their five little ones. Her conversation was filled with colics and teething fevers. She had no interest in balls, parties or flirting. What did she see in her husband? He was as ugly as a cottager's jug.

"I hate them, and they hate me," reflected Jane, without a hint of regret. And Wally would grow up with a poor opinion of his mother.

"Do you need anything, Madam?" asked Babs, the housemaid who also acted as her personal maid. She was gossipy and knew other maids in other houses bigger and grander than this one, and brought her mistress any news she had gleaned about the comings and goings of the gentry, for which she was rewarded with cast-offs and baubles.

"Brush my hair, Babs."

"Certainly, Madam." Babs took up the hairbrush and began to work, and as she worked, she praised.

"Not one grey hair, Madam!"

"Well Babs, I am still under thirty."

"Oh yes, Madam, but there are twenty-three-year-olds I 'ave seen with a grey hair or two!"

"I see you're off tomorrow afternoon, are you going anywhere?" Jane wanted to change the subject.

"Yes, Madam. I'm meeting my friend who has just got a new place, I'm going over to the house, for a look-see, just to see where she works."

"That's exciting, Babs. I do wish I could just go for look-sees. But I have to be invited, unless there is a new female in the neighbourhood, then I may call upon that person quite properly."

"Oh, Madam, there will be somebody new in the neighbourhood soon! Actually, not really in this neighbourhood exactly, but here in Chelsea."

"Will there? Who, and where?"

"It's a Mr. *Song Sane*. A widower I believe—"

"*Song Sane*! What a peculiar name!"

"It's spelled S-A-I-N-T S-A-E-N-S though, Madam, with a bar between the Song and the Sane."

"Saint-Saens! I suppose he's a foreigner? Oh, my! And is he old?"

"Not old, Madam. But 'e's an Englishman, not a foreigner."

"He sounds—noble. So, where does this Mr. Saint-Saens live?"

"I heard that he's on the continent, but that Rockwell Park will be got ready for him before he returns."

"Rockwell! But that's the biggest house for many miles! He must be very rich!"

"Oh yes, I believe so, Madam. There's to be a staff of seven men to do the grounds. I suppose there will be twenty or thirty servants."

I hope he returns soon. Jane thought as she climbed into bed a little while later. *A wealthy widower, only a short distance off! I shall have to contrive to meet him, somehow or another.*

She lay awake, having run out of her sleeping elixir. Her thoughts were always horrid when she lay awake in the dark. Memories flew out of dark corners of her mind, like bats. She could not control them, could not catch them and put them back. She opened the drawer of her bedside table and took out a small bottle. She drank half of the gin-bottle and was asleep very soon.

CHAPTER TWENTY-NINE

SALTWICK ISLAND

Summer on Saltwick was tragic, as Billy Foster and young Harry Beasley drowned while fishing when a squall blew up. Billy left a wife and two small children, and Harry was the second boy in his family to drown.

In July, disaster struck for the second year in a row. The fish died and floated in the river, in a frothy bath of red liquid. A new textile mill had opened on the bank of the Wick upstream and was discharging its dyes into the river. The islanders were hungry, and it was not even winter yet. The potato crop, though not as bad as last year's, was not healthy, yielding puny vegetables. It would be insufficient to sustain them for the lean months.

The King and Dr. Gibson led a delegation of six men to the textile mill, but got no satisfaction from the owner, who said that it was not his factory that had done the damage, but another further up the river Wick. This factory blamed the first one, and their complaining was a waste of time. The islanders expected no better from 'the World' and returned even more convinced that it was a very evil place.

They prepared for another grim winter, and the men had no choice but to go away again for work.

"What shall we do?" asked Gwen.

The response took her greatly by surprise.

"We'll go to the workhouse for the winter," said Aunt Nuru.

"Auntie, we might die in the workhouse!"

"We'll die if we don't."

"But Auntie, what about the withies?"

"We'll harvest them afore we go."

"We'll come back, won't we? In the spring?"

"We'll come back. Of course, we'll come back. We have to make the baskets."

"What do people take to the workhouse?"

"Nothing at all, because if you do, they'll tell you that you aren't destitute. We'll go in our oldest clothes, and you wear your old boots, the ones with the toes coming out. You'll get better ones to wear in the workhouse."

The day came. Carrying only a small bundle each, they said goodbye to their cabin and their neighbours. They had buried Rascal the winter before. They were rowed over.

As they walked in the December rain toward the workhouse, Gwen remembered how she had been taken to a workhouse by her mother eight years ago. Her memories were hazy—was it here, or in London? Would she remember the wall, the gates, the man at the door? It was coming back to her and she dragged her feet, her feet pinched, and wet from the gaping boot-toes.

Nuru was silent. There had been a change in her that Gwen did not like to see. Sometimes she feared that Nuru was ill; she coughed a great deal and held her side. Harvesting the withies had worn her out.

Gwen could not tell if this workhouse was the same place or not that she had been taken to before, but if not, it was very like. They were admitted by the porter, taken to a building, and baths were run by two women who were brisk and efficient. Their own clothes were taken away, and they were given ugly, scratchy gowns to wear, with pinafores. Then Nuru said goodbye to her and went one way.

"You're in the Girls' Section," she was told. "We'll take you over there now. It's just teatime."

Gwen felt almost sick with fright when the saw the Hall full of hundreds of girls aged about seven to fifteen sitting at tables. They all wore the same uniform. They all talked. She wanted to turn and run.

"Well go on, don't you want to eat then? Sit there," the woman half-pushed her to a place on a long bench. The others made room for her.

The noise, the darkness of the Hall, with small beams of light showing in through windows that were narrow and high, everybody hemmed in, the smell of something cooking, combined with stale smells from the walls and the very furniture, made her feel distressed and short of breath. Her heart began to race faster and faster, causing her to feel faint. Her face began to feel ice-cold; her hands trembled. The chatter around her became an unbearable *thrum-thrum-thrum* in her ears. She could not breathe; her throat, her lungs seemed to have closed down. Her heart hammered loudly as if it had moved to her ears. Without even knowing what she was doing, she jumped up, startling her neighbours; and leaping over the bench, ran for the door as if for her life, only to be stopped by two of the attendants.

"What are you doing? You have to eat your supper!"

She fell against the door.

"Let me out!" she managed to say, though having to gasp every word. "I want—to go home! I can't breathe—I can't breathe! I'm dying!" She meant what she said, she was sure that she was living her last few moments on earth. A feeling of impending doom swept through her like the wind blows through a room with an open window. The world seemed to be going away; she was conscious of a swirling before her eyes. When had she felt like this before? She remembered Rush Pier and slid to the floor.

One attendant shouted for the doctor, and they dragged her outside and laid her down on the stone steps. She began to feel a little recovered, her heart slowed a little, and she felt the blood returning to her face. It was a few minutes before she was able to talk.

"So many people in there … I couldn't breathe!" she spoke in gasps.

The doctor came, hurrying. He knelt beside her and took her pulse while the women described what had happened.

"It's only an attack of hysteria," he said. "Where are you from, girl?"

"Saltwick Island."

"I should have guessed. You islanders are wild creatures in a cage. You cannot stand it."

"There shouldn't be anybody livin' on that island anymore. Everybody who comes from there is mad," the tall attendant remarked.

This remark caused Gwen to cry out.

"Becky, you shouldn't 'ave said that!" lectured the shorter attendant. "Shall we take her up to the dormitory, Doctor, and let 'er sup there tonight?"

"No indeed. She must go back inside."

"No!" cried Gwen, covering her mouth as if she were about to be sick.

"Come on, I insist." He pulled her to her feet. "I will walk with you to your place. You will be all right. You will not die. Do you hear me? *You will not die.*"

There was something in his tone that reassured her.

He steered her in. Grace had just been said. The attendant showed him where to lead her and she stepped awkwardly over the bench between the two other girls, who gave each other a smirk, and sat down. She felt a little nervous still, but mostly she felt very weak, and very, very tired.

He patted her shoulder and leaned his head to her ear.

"You will be all right now," he said firmly. "Eat your supper."

A bowl of soup was in front of her and a hunk of bread and cheese. She obeyed. The girls on either side of her were sniggering. What horrible people there were here in the World! Where was Aunt Nuru? Why were they not allowed to be in the same house?

After supper, prayers were said and then it was time for bed. The attendant told her to follow the girls who were at her table. A different attendant in the dormitory upstairs showed her her bed.

She had to share it with another girl. But she was so tired, she slept very deeply.

CHAPTER THIRTY

For several days Gwen was miserable. The other girls, hearing that she was a *Saltwicker,* looked down on her and laughed at her. Led by a girl named Tess, a pock-marked girl small for her age but the leader of six or seven girls, they mocked her speech and thrust books into her hand to read, knowing that she had never learned. The girl she shared the bed with, Nellie, ignored her and seemed embarrassed to be saddled with her.

Worst of all, she was required to attend school, and was put in with the seven-year-olds who were learning their ABCs. But her teacher was a kind lady who took time with her and told her that if she applied herself, she could catch up quickly. Miss Ancoats also discovered that she had poor sight, and sent her to the doctor, who sent her out to another doctor, who prescribed spectacles. Instead of making her happy that she could see better, Gwen thought she looked ugly in them and she endured more ridicule from Tess and her friends.

Gwen had one thought and one only—she wanted to go home. On Sunday, after Church and dinner, their mothers were allowed to visit them.

Nuru came into the Hall and embraced her. They sat close together and Gwen immediately poured out everything on her heart.

"Oh dear, I never thought to warn you," Nuru reproached herself for the dining hall incident. "I should've told you there'd be a swarm of people! It 'appened to Daffy too, I shoulda remembered!"

"The girls are horrid," whispered Gwen.

"They'll be even more horrid tonight," said Nuru, "when they've seen you with me."

It was true. The girls teased her that night about her 'mother' who was dark-skinned. Gwen shed the bitterest tears she had ever shed in her life into her pillow, drenching it while the dormitory slept.

The following day, a girl with long dark plaits who

had never joined in the teasing, walked with her over to the school.

"Don't mind Tess and them," she said. "It was the same when I came. It's 'orrible to watch some of them being nasty to new girls, when they themselves were teased when they came. Look, will you be my friend, Gwen? My name is Jenny. I'll 'elp you with your readin'."

Gwen was happy to say 'yes' as they parted at the schoolroom door. At last, a ray of hope in this miserable place!

She still did not like the crowds in the dining hall, but at least she could sit and eat without fear of another hysterical attack, even though she still felt very nervous and uncomfortable. The food was not bad, but there was almost no fish.

Jenny was true to her word. She helped her to learn.

"Is that really your mother?" she asked her one Sunday after she saw her with Nuru. She herself had no visitors.

"No," said Gwen with some awkwardness. "She adopted me when I was six."

That led to more questions, and Gwen told her what

had happened. Jenny was horrified that she had almost been murdered.

"What of you, then?" Gwen asked her.

"I never knew a mother's love neither," Jenny said. "I was born 'ere and my mother left me 'ere. You were lucky to find a mother's love though it wasn't from your own mother."

Gwen was silent. She'd been feeling so sorry for herself and had not realised that Jenny had suffered also. She looked about at the other girls, wondering about them.

"Nellie didn't have no mother neither." Jenny said, seeing her eyes wander. "She was left at the porter's gate after being born. Tess came in about two years ago, covered in sores, and bone-thin. They thought she was going to die."

"Tess!"

"When she came first, she was in a bad way. There was a big girl here at the time who used to trip 'er all the time an' make her cry."

"Why is Tess nasty to new girls now?"

"I don't know! I often wondered that too."

As Jenny told her the circumstances of every girl's admission to the workhouse, Gwen began to feel sorry for all of them. Even the worst teases, the most cruel ones, like Tess, had suffered.

CHAPTER THIRTY-ONE

"Gwendoline Paul." The Matron came into the Hall one cold frosty morning as they were queuing for breakfast. Gwen suddenly felt all eyes upon her, and blushed. What was the matter? She raised her hand with reluctance.

"Come with me, please." Gwen stepped out of the row and followed the starchy woman as she led the way along a hallway and into a small office.

"Sit down," Matron said. Gwen sat gingerly on the edge of a chair. She was frightened of Matron, of her power. She was the ultimate authority in the Girls' and Women's Section, and had never addressed her before.

But Matron was looking at her kindly.

"I am sorry to give you bad news," she said, her voice dropping to a low tone. "Your guardian, Mrs. Nuru Paul, has died."

Gwen could not take in the words Matron was saying. She looked at her with blankness. After a time, the truth began to sink into her mind. She slumped in her chair, not crying, but deathly white. The shock numbed her through and through.

Matron rang a bell, and a nurse came in. She was taken to the Infirmary where she was put into a bed. She stayed there for the day, staring at the ceiling in total shock, unable to think, unable to cry. Over the next few days, she began to understand her new reality and wept. Aunt Nuru was buried before she left the infirmary, in a pauper's grave.

At least the girls left her alone now. They seemed sympathetic and treated her gently. After a week had passed, Matron called her to her office again.

"Mrs. Paul, poor soul, told me about how you came to be with her," she said. "She thought that you should try to find your Aunt. Your real Aunt."

"But I want to go back to Saltwick! In the spring!"

"You cannot go back there, Gwendoline. There's nothing for you there. It's a terrible place. And how would you keep yourself? In any case, you're not of age to make the decision about how to decide your life. The Board of Guardians must decide what's best for you. Can you remember your Aunt's name, and where she lived?"

Gwen squirmed. "I don't want to go back. My mother—" She bit her lip.

"Your mother, when she is found, will have a visit from the police, and they will determine if there is a case to be answered."

Gwen shook her head.

"I don't want to be the cause of my mother being hanged!"

"It's out of your hands, Gwendoline. Justice must be served. The Board are very determined; in fact, they have already made a report. You mustn't be frightened, Gwendoline. The police will come and see you next week."

"Next week?" Gwen raised her head, turning her eyes upon the Matron. To herself she said: *I am leaving this place tonight.*

CHAPTER THIRTY-TWO

After lights-out, Gwen stayed awake for a long time. She got up and put her clothes and boots on very quietly, over her nightgown. She put on her spectacles. She had no possessions, so there was nothing for her to carry. She had no shawl, coat or bonnet.

She tiptoed to the door of the dormitory and turned the knob. To her great disappointment, it was locked. They were on the third floor of the building and the windows were high up in the room. It was impossible.

But tomorrow was Sunday. They were marched to the village church for Sunday Service. Could she slip away on her way there, or back?

She'd have to confide in Jenny, because she usually

walked with her. They'd have to be at the end of the line, and she would have to pretend she didn't notice. The good thing about this plan is that she would have her coat and bonnet.

Money. She had none. It could not be helped! She'd get back to Saltwick somehow!

The next morning, she drew Jenny aside and told her. She was upset but agreed that it was the only thing to be done. They went to Church, and on their way back, in the frosty churchyard, she and Jenny managed to form the last two in line as they began their march back to the workhouse. Jenny took out her prayer-book and was absorbed by it. As they passed a part of the road where there was a copse of trees, Gwen held back and stepped into it. Screened by the trees, she ran and ran, deeper into the trees which she knew, from her many visits to the town, gave onto another road that led directly to the railway station.

But she knew now she could not go back to Saltwick, even if there were boats out, coming and going from Rush Pier. The police might look for her there, and the islanders did not like the police. But she wasn't safe at the railway station either. She would just sit in the waiting room for warmth for a little while and think about what to do next.

I shall have to take my chances on the public road, she said to herself, jumping up and setting out. Her orphan's uniform would give her away, so she resolved to keep her coat on at all times. She walked briskly but did not run.

There wasn't much travel on Sundays, so she walked for a long time on the London road before a cart stopped to ask her if she wanted a lift. He was a kind-looking old farmer with two children beside him—a safe prospect. She hopped on and he took her five miles. After that, she was very hungry and went to an Inn, hoping to beg for food. She took her spectacles off as she was sure that any description that went out would have her wearing them.

"You're full young to be out on yer own," remarked the cook at the back door. "But 'ere, I 'ave a few potatoes left over." She handed them to her in a piece of torn newspaper.

The sun was going down now. Gwen began to shiver. She saw an old barn and slipped in when the stable hand was not looking, and going to the back, made a little nest of straw where she fell asleep. She was upon her way before the sun was up the following morning, and as it was Monday, many travellers were about. She was nearing the

Metropolis, and traffic increased. More houses, more towns. Saltwick was further and further away with every mile. She drank from public pumps and begged again at the back door of an Inn, this time receiving bread and cheese on her third attempt, after being shooed away at the first two.

By nightfall, she was in London! There was no danger of her being found now! Her first task was to get some new clothes, but for that she would have to get help. The only person she could think of was Aunt Ellen.

She made her way to the Docklands. It was a large place, she knew. But how to find her aunt? She did not even remember her surname, or the name of the street where she lived! It was a red-brick, terraced house with a vegetable shop opposite. She remembered something very useful—twin boys, Hector and Charlie, four years younger than she. They'd be ten now. Where would she begin?

CHAPTER THIRTY-THREE

Though she was homeless, hungry and had lived in the same clothes for days now, Gwen felt a sense of freedom she had not experienced since the day she had left Saltwick. She walked around the parks and went to London Bridge, leaning out to look at the river. How she loved the water! To think that this same body of water would take her to the Estuary, to the Wick and then to Saltwick Island! She took off her spectacles the better to feel the air on her face, though the smells of the city spoiled it somewhat. She was free of the workhouse, free of the discipline of the bells, free of the stuffy, horrible Hall where she'd thought she was dying! The only thing she missed was the food; bad as it was, it was regular and filled her stomach. And Jenny. She could read a little now, thanks to Miss Ancoats and Jenny.

"I say, Miss, lookin' for a bit o'fun?" the low-toned male voice close to her ear startled her. She put on her spectacles hurriedly as she turned around, and the middle-aged man hurried away, muttering *'Blimey, a bluestocking!'* Gwen giggled. She did not like her spectacles, but they might be useful in keeping trouble away.

Hector and Charlie, Hector and Charlie. She enquired for her cousins wherever she saw a group of youngsters and was almost giving up hope when a boy piped up that he knew Hector and Charlie! They were the Terrible Twins. Everybody knew Hector and Charlie!

The boy knew where they lived and gave her directions. How often she must have walked these streets with Aunt Ellen, but she recognised very little! When she turned the corner into Eastgate Row, her memories returned—the long narrow street, with terraced houses on one side and shops on the other. And there was the vegetable shop. She turned her steps to Number 47.

The door was answered by a man older and shorter than she remembered—her uncle?

"I'm Gwendoline, come back." she announced herself.

"Gwendoline!" his voice seemed soft and wondering as he held out his hand. "Gwendoline Compton come back! Come in, come in!" she followed him into the living room. It was dark and shabby and held no memories for her. "Ellen!" he called into another room. "Gwendoline's come back to see us."

A great flurry, hurried footsteps, and her aunt, older also, rushed out to greet her. They embraced with warmth.

"Where have you been all these years? Why din't you write?"

Gwen took off her coat to show her blue striped workhouse uniform.

"In the workhouse all this time! That's 'orrid, that is. And you're very thin. Before you ask, I don't know where your mother is. She and I parted company for good that day she took you from here. I don't know how much you remember. She was supposed to take you 'ome, to her 'ome—but she said she was going to take you to the workhouse instead."

"She did, and they wouldn't take me. They said I wasn't destitute. They sent us away."

"What happened then?"

Gwen looked down at the hearthrug. An uneasy quiet fell upon the room as she searched for the words.

"What 'appened? Where did you grow up, Gwen?"

"I grew up in Saltwick Island, a little island in the Wick River, that runs into the Thames near the Estuary." Mention of the island made her a little tearful, for Andy, and Nuru and Betty and the fresh sea air. For the life that was gone from her.

"I never 'eard of it," her uncle mused. "I never even 'eard of the Wick!"

"It's very small and hidden away. I lived with a family there named Paul. I go by Paul. I lived there until Uncle Andy died. Then Auntie Nuru and I went into the workhouse. So I've only been in the workhouse a short time, you see? Auntie Nuru died a few weeks ago." Tears came into her eyes.

"I can see you were fond of this Nuru," said Ellen. "Funny name, in't it? Is it a nickname?"

"No, Nuru's descended from Africans."

The couple looked at her strangely.

"But how did your mother set you up with 'em? How did she find 'em?"

"She didn't find them. They found me."

"She abandoned you?" said Uncle Oswald, leaning forward, his eyes alight.

"Oh, worse than that. She drugged me and threw me into the river. I was rescued."

A terrible silence followed this statement.

"No," said Ellen firmly. "You're lying. You 'ave a fanciful imagination. You're lying."

Gwen was completely taken aback at this accusation.

"It's true!"

"No, I won't hear this slur against Jane! She has 'er faults, but she's not a murderess."

Ellen got up and walked about the room. Finally she turned around.

"I must ask you to leave, Gwen."

Gwen paled.

"Why don't you believe me?" she said. "The island people know the truth, the men who rescued me saw 'er run away! Even a milk-woman knew there was something odd about 'er!"

"No, not my own sister, not a Compton. You're not welcome here, Gwen. Out you go, now!"

"Wait, wait," said Oswald, as Gwen's eyes became hot with tears. "I always said your sister was a bad seed. I want to 'ear more."

"Please let me stay. I have no food, money nor even a change of clothes. I—I was hoping you would help me." Gwen stammered. "I ran away from the workhouse, because before Auntie Nuru died, she told the Board of Guardians about my mother and they are going to get the police. I don't want Mother to hang, bad as she is, for attempted murder. I don't want to have her hanging on my conscience! I never told anybody this address, I'd forgot it in fact, and only found the house through remembering the twins' names."

Something in her manner seemed to ring true with Aunt Ellen, who sat down again. "Of course, you can stop, for a while, until you get yourself settled. But don't say another word about what 'appened that day. I din't want to let you go, Gwen! It was 'im!" She threw her arm toward her husband, who looked very uncomfortable.

"I thought she was going to Bullmere," he protested. "If I'd a-known—"

"Tha's enough! I don't want to go back to tha' day!"

She began to weep.

CHAPTER THIRTY-FOUR

Gwen was relieved to exchange her workhouse uniform for an old gown of Aunt Ellen's. It was too large, but she did not mind. Her little cousins tumbled into the house later on. Hector and Charlie! They did not know her at all, of course, and seemed very uninterested in this stranger. They ate a supper of bread and bacon and tea.

Uncle Oswald only worked sporadically, and he and Aunt Ellen now only had the downstairs part of the house. The twins slept in a small room off the living room, and Gwen was given this room, while they slept on the hearthrug in front of the fire. It was obvious to her that she could not stay for very long. She would have to find work soon. But what could she do?

Uncle Oswald brought home a newspaper and placed it in front of her. *"Servants Wanted,* see?" He pointed the section out to her.

"I can't read that," said Gwen. "The words are too big and hard, I don't know what it says."

"You never learned to read! What kind of a place was that Saltwick? Was there no school?"

"No." Gwen felt very uncomfortable, and defensive of Saltwick. "The King didn't believe in education."

"The King!" Her aunt and uncle chorused and burst into laughter.

"Will he march soon at the head of an army to take over the whole of England?" said Oswald, guffawing.

"And Scotland! What kind of an army 'as he got, Gwen?" her aunt almost collapsed in hysterics.

"Cavalry and Lancers!" chortled her uncle.

Gwen flushed deeply and saw and felt acutely the chasm between her and her relations, as wide as the Thames Estuary itself. She did not know these people. But she had no option but to endure it, until Aunt Ellen at last noticed her downcast eyes and trembling lip.

"Oh, do come on Gwen, take a joke!" she said, wiping her eyes with the corner of her apron. "We don't mean any 'arm, but really, the King of Saltwick!" she burst into chuckles again, in spite of her trying not to.

"I haven't laughed so much in years!" Uncle Oswald, oblivious to Gwen's feelings, was still enjoying himself.

I don't belong here, Gwen thought. *I don't belong anywhere except in Saltwick. I want to go back to my people there! I'm going back there someday. Yes, I will! But I need money to do that. I need to find work. I'll save, so that before I go back, I can buy a store of food and fuel to keep me for the winter. I won't need much.*

"Uncle, will you please read me out the notices for *Servants Wanted*?" she asked with dignity, raising her chin, trying to control her tears. "I want to get a place as soon as ever I can."

CHAPTER THIRTY-FIVE

THE ENGLISH CHANNEL

The ship had not long left Calais when there was a knock on the stateroom door. Mr. Saint-Saens got up to answer it, but the valet was quicker.

"A card for you, sir," said Latour, placing it on a silver tray to present to his master, though he was only two feet away. "I told the steward to wait for an answer." Latour evidently knew the contents.

Mr. Saint-Saens took the envelope and opened it.

It was an invitation to dine with the Captain. He frowned a little. He wasn't very easy in company, and preferred to dine alone. But Marie's words came back to him.

Why are you so reserved, darling, when everybody likes you?

"Tell the Captain I shall be happy to join him," he said to Latour, who conveyed the information to the steward waiting at the door six feet away.

Mr. Saint-Saens asked for his cloak and hat and went on deck. He had not been to England for many years. But it was time to return now. Marie had suffered from sea-sickness and could not accompany him, and he had not wanted to leave her, so his family had come to see him in France instead.

Marie! Marie! He missed her acutely, so deeply that he felt he would never be happy again, and never love again as he had loved her. He placed his gloved hands on the rail and looked out at the choppy grey sea taking him away from his home of the last six years.

Marie had loved him from the very week he had taken up employment in the large stately home in Normandy, though he had not known that detail until they had become engaged. She'd been twenty-one and the mistress of her father's grand house in the countryside. He had been tutor to her little brother who was too unwell to attend school.

Marie had many suitors, but never became engaged.

He thought that she was too particular. The housekeeper, gossiping, had said that her heart could not be easily won. Her father had received many offers for her, but she had refused all, even from very wealthy, titled men.

He had found out the reason for her continued rejections one astonishing evening soon after little Henri's funeral. He had no reason to stay now and was preparing to leave. He was packing and she came to his room. He was very startled. What was she doing here? He'd been a little cold and distant.

She'd stood before him, petite Marie, in her black mourning silk, with her large brown eyes fixed on his. She wrung her hands. She could not bear the thought of his leaving. He must not go! It was heartbreaking to lose Henri, and now—was she to lose him also?

This much of the conversation was at the door. "Please allow me to come in," she begged.

"Of course," he said, a little embarrassed.

She did not hesitate in her words.

"The fact is, Monsieur, that I love you. I have loved you almost from the time we met, that first day, when I took you to Henri. You were so good to him, from the first! He was happier in your care than with anybody before, and you have become part of the family. I had to tell you before you go, so that you can tell me that it is no use, or that I have—hope." she bit her lip. She was being very forward.

"You love me? But I am only a tutor." he said, astonished to hear her words. Yes, he admired her, and liked her, and had thought that the lucky suitor would have a gem, but he had never allowed himself to even think beyond that. Aristocratic young ladies do not marry their brothers' tutors, and after he had given of himself so freely before, only to be deeply hurt, he had his heart well under control.

"Why do you think I have never married, and sent all those men away? Who sent you a verse for your birthday? Who sent you the Valentine?"

"I thought it was—one of the maids," he said with awkwardness. "Though I thought the notepaper was particularly fine for a maid. It came into my head that it could have been you, but I dismissed it. It was you!"

"Have you ever seen me as a woman you could love, Monsieur, if, for instance, I were a mere maid?"

He smiled and pushed back the lock of hair that fell over his brow.

"If you were a maid, and I was sure of your affections, I would have perhaps allowed myself to attach—but Mademoiselle, you are not a maid, and I would never aspire—your father would make a very strenuous objection—" he said, his thoughts and feelings rather jumbled.

"Father knows how I feel for you. I told him just an hour ago, when I began to be afraid that you would leave! Father wants my happiness! Do you feel nothing for me?"

There was a little warning bell in his mind, but this situation was different to the one so long ago, the one that had broken his heart. Marie was humble, sincere, kind. Marie would not pretend love.

"Do you feel nothing for me?" she repeated, putting her hands out but not daring to touch him.

"I think you are the most lovable woman in the world!" he burst out suddenly. Her eyes brimmed over with tears and he grasped her hands and they kissed, chastely.

"Then we will be married?" she said, beaming. "Oh, please ask me! I want you to ask me!"

He got down on one knee and took her hand.

"Mademoiselle Marie, I love you dearly. Will you do me the great honour of becoming my wife?"

"Yes, yes!" she wept.

They shared another kiss before she hurried away, her eyes filled with tears of joy. He unpacked his things again, slowly, as if in a dream. The feelings he had chased away for years took life. He knew in his heart that they would be happy.

The following morning, he dressed in his Sunday best and knocked on her father's door. The old man told him that he trusted his daughter completely to him. He had seen him to be a man of excellent character, sincere affection, temperate in his habits and free of pride and avarice. There was just one thing he would ask of him.

The Saint-Saens were an old and noble family. It was sometimes required that when a man from a non-aristocratic family married into a noble line, he would change his name, so that the name would be carried on. Would he be willing to surrender his birth name, to take on that of Saint-Saens?

Mr. Brown knew that this was expected, and he agreed. After the family came out of mourning, he and Marie were married. The old man died soon after the wedding. Marie did not survive him by two years. She died giving birth to their daughter, Marie Louise. It was an utter heartbreak, and for months, Jack thought that he would die of grief. He saw nobody for eight weeks after the funeral, but constantly roamed the woods near his home, struggling to understand, thinking and praying with a heart in smithereens. Only the thought of his little girl sustained him. She was the apple of his eye.

Mr. Saint-Saens, formerly Mr. Jack Brown, inherited a large fortune. He was very wealthy but would have parted with every centime to have Marie back. He was not interested in wealth. It was only given to him by God to do good to others.

He was going back to England to raise his daughter nearer to his own family. She was with him on board ship, in another cabin with her nurse and a nursery maid. He went now to that cabin and his heart lifted when she toddled toward him, crying "Papa! Papa!" her arms outstretched to be lifted up. He swung her in his arms and whirled her about, laughing. The nurse watched him, a soft look in her eye. How this Papa loved his little girl!

CHAPTER THIRTY-SIX

The Captain's other tablemates were his officers and another English gentleman named Mr. Basil Barrett-Smith. He was a young man, about twenty-two years old, returning from his European Tour, and with reluctance.

"I was in Monte Carlo when I got word from my old man. He wants me home to take over the running of the estate," he said. "I would rather have stayed to recoup some losses I took there, and my friends were very upset that I couldn't stay. But I had to answer the summons. Our tenant farmers are in an uproar. I daresay I shall get used to it all."

"Where are your estates, Mr. Barrett-Smith?" asked the first officer.

"In Essex, bordering the Thames Estuary."

"You are an old family, then?" asked the Captain.

"We are indeed, sir."

"And you, Mr. Saint-Saens? An old family also? I will wager your ancestors came to England as far back as the Norman Invasion, and roundly defeated us at Hastings. My name, as you know, is Godwin. But I will not hold the victory against you!"

Jack did not contradict him, only to smile and say: "Definitely Norman, Captain."

"And your seat is—?"

"I have no land in England, Captain, at the present time, except a house recently purchased in Town by an agent. It is called Rockwell, and it is situated in Chelsea."

"Rockwell! In Chelsea!" Mr. Barrett-Smith said, in an excited tone. "I know it! It is quite a pile, sir. I visited it when I was sixteen or so. The Ashtons were in residence then, and their son was a schoolfellow. I spent an Easter there. An extensive property, set on a height, with woods behind, and overlooking the Thames. Not far from the house inhabited by the noted Tudor Chancellor Thomas More. The Park stretches all the way to Queen Anne Road. You have not seen it?"

"My agent sent a drawing he had made. It is a gracious place, and its appeal for me was the privacy of the woods and extensive, well-kept garden for my daughter. My mother, who has been living many years with my brother Robert and his family in Bath, has offered to come and keep house for us, and it is for her I wished a well-established garden also."

"Neither you nor your mother will be disappointed, sir, when you set foot in Rockwell. If I'm not being too forward, I should dearly love to see it again. I daresay my father will manacle me to our own estate for quite a time, though!"

"You will be very welcome to visit at any time, sir," said Jack.

"Will it be staffed, sir, upon your arrival?" asked the second officer.

"I believe so. My mother has seen to it."

CHAPTER THIRTY-SEVEN

C

HELSEA

"Madam, I have the girl I spoke of to you, for interview." said Mrs. Higgins, the housekeeper of Rockwell to her new mistress, the elderly and, she thought, slightly befuddled Mrs. Brown.

"Thank you, Mrs. Higgins. I will see her."

"If I might be permitted to say, Madam, I would be reluctant to employ this girl."

"Why so, Mrs. Higgins?"

"She comes with no references or characters. She grew up on an island, and then spent some time in a workhouse before coming to London. I suppose the only thing in her favour, Madam, is that she wears spectacles, and so not likely to attract followers."

"I will see her, Mrs. Higgins."

"As you say, Madam." Mrs. Higgins left the drawing room and entered the servant stairwell, where she beckoned to the terrified girl standing at the foot of the steps.

Mrs. Brown arranged her hands on her lap. Recently arrived from Bath, she had been very busy setting the house in order for her son and granddaughter. He had sent her detailed instructions—he was so particular, was Jack! Always wanting to do good to people deprived of opportunity! So particular was she to carry out her son's wishes that instead of allowing Mrs. Higgins to engage even the most junior maids, she was interviewing them herself.

Jack's rise to fortune had been astonishing, but it would not spoil him—no, Jack's heart was in the right place. He was a good boy. Too good for the world, she often thought, and Robert was convinced that his soft heart was too easily swayed. He saw no evil in anybody. He wanted to do good with his fortune. She had his letter in front of her on the table.

Mother, if you could see your way to engaging some poor

or destitute people, it is what I would like. I will leave it up to your discretion, but if you could get some boys and girls from a workhouse, for instance, I would like to see that they got a chance. As you know they are often apprenticed to the worst places, where they are neglected, and any schooling they have had is soon forgotten.

Jack was passionate about schooling.

Now here was a girl who qualified according to Jack's directions. She said, "Come in!" to the timid knock on the door.

The girl came into the drawing room, and Mrs. Brown surveyed her. She was thin, and wore very shabby clothes too large for her frame—quite shabby enough for Jack to be content. Her fair hair was a little wild, with strands poking out from her bonnet, framing her pale face with untidy strands. Behind the round spectacles, her eyes were wide with fright. The child had probably never in her life seen a room like this.

"Come closer," Mrs. Brown said pleasantly, again, for the child named Paul had advanced only a foot inside the door.

"What is your Christian name, child?"

"Gwendoline, Ma'am."

"How old are you, Gwendoline?"

"Fifteen, Ma'am."

"Are your mother and father living?"

"They are dead, Ma'am."

"I'm sorry to hear it. Have you brothers and sisters?"

The girl shook her head.

"You grew up where?"

"In Saltwick Island, Ma'am."

"Where is that?"

"On the River Wick, Ma'am."

"Did you ever learn cookery?"

"Oh yes, Ma'am. I can gut a fish and clean it and have it on the pan in five minutes. Just give me a chance, Ma'am, is all I ask. Do you like fish, Ma'am?"

Mrs. Brown could not but smile at the sudden eagerness.

"If I take you on, will you work hard here? We'll train you in the kitchen. If you're very good, you can be promoted, in time. You must take your orders from Mrs. Leonard, the Cook. We expect honesty, neatness of person and courtesy at all times. We'll pay you ten pounds a year, paid quarterly. That's generous, but the Master of the house, my son, is a good, generous man."

"Yes, Ma'am. I am so grateful, Ma'am!" Miss Paul curtsied. *Ten pounds a year*, she said to herself. *Will I even need to stay a year?*

"Run along now, and ask Mrs. Higgins to come in."

That lady was hovering by the door and was resigned to the fact that her advice had not been taken. What other ragamuffins would be taken off the street because Mr. Saint-Saens fancied this house to be a charitable institution? Yet, she was somewhat pleased that Mr. Saint-Saens had a good, honest, Christian character. She too was grateful for those who had given her a chance.

Leonora Higgins had been the daughter of a jeweller who had lost everything from an unwise investment. Her mother had died young and she had kept house for her father from the age of fourteen. Her father died when she was nineteen, a broken man, leaving no means of support for his daughter. She had hired herself out as a governess, but had not liked the confines of the schoolroom, and as she was skilled in housekeeping, had worked for a time in a house of middling size, and another a little bigger and then had applied for this situation. Mrs. Brown had taken a liking to her bright, open expression and her declaration that in spite of her youth, she was well able to run a tight ship, but would take care also that Downstairs was a happy, harmonious place. It was a large household, but she was a shrewd, intelligent woman and learned quickly. She hoped that she was set for life now; she was in her mid-thirties, and would never marry. The title 'Mrs.' was honourific.

CHAPTER THIRTY-EIGHT

Gwen could hardly believe her great fortune. This was only the third place she had tried, and it was by far the grandest. Rockwell, with its majesty and grandeur both enthralled and terrified her. Mrs. Brown had seemed nice, but she was as grand as Royalty, and Gwen might as well have been in the presence of the Queen, with the fright and awe she felt. Mrs. Higgins had a stern look. She wore a black frilled mobcap, a black gown with a violet shawl caught in a bejewelled clasp in the front, and a loop of chain hung about her waist, upon which she carried several keys, a set of small vials and a little scissors.

Gwen followed her up a narrow staircase to the top of the house, and down a long hallway to a small room with three beds crammed next to each other, a narrow wardrobe, and a chest of drawers upon which rested a jug and basin of water next to a towel rail. There was no fireplace.

"You're sharing with Peggy and Madge. Here's a drawer to put your things. Keep them neat and tidy. I do inspections. You will rise at five-thirty every morning. The other maids will show you what to do. The Mistress has provided uniforms. Here is yours, hanging up ready. It may be too big for you, but you'll grow into it, and anyway you'll be out of sight downstairs. Brush your hair back under your cap, I don't want to see a strand showing, not one. Be downstairs in five minutes in your uniform with clean face and hands. I will wait for you at the bottom of the servants' staircase. Will you be able to find your way?"

"Yes, Mrs. Higgins." Gwen began to get a morose feeling that this was like the workhouse. She was already feeling hemmed in and anxious. But she had to earn money to buy enough supplies to sustain her for next winter on Saltwick, so she had to stick it out.

CHAPTER THIRTY-NINE

Gwen lost her way trying to go downstairs. She ended up in a hallway with another stairs at the end of it, and when she took this, found it led to a back door to the outside. She turned and became completely lost.

"Hey-day, who are you?" said a male voice.

"I'm Gwen Paul, the new maid, and I got lost trying to find the kitchen."

"Jeremy Markham at your service, Gwen. I will take you there. Follow me." said the tall, thin footman with straight black eyebrows and prominent chin.

"Mrs. Higgins will be very annoyed. She's waiting for me at the bottom of the servants' staircase."

Mr. Markham burst into laughter as he led her

down another hallway, past rooms where each one had a window that looked out on the hall. She could see maids ironing and folding sheets, and in another room, two maids were busy doing something with bottles and jars.

"Oh, don't mind 'er."

"What do you do here?"

"I'm second footman. A very important job. I have to leave you now and polish a pair of boots."

"That's why you're called a footman."

He turned on her, but seeing that she was not being smart, he smirked.

"I do a lot more than polish boots. The kitchen is that way."

"Thank you, Mr. Markham."

She espied Mrs. Higgins bearing down on one of the rooms and apologised for getting lost.

"You'll get used to the house in time," was her reply. She looked her up and down with a critical eye and seemed satisfied. "Peggy! Take the new girl with you, show her the scullery."

"Is this my new scullery maid, then?" said a large

woman with a round face, busy mixing dough as they passed through the kitchen.

"This is Gwen. Gwen, this is Mrs. Leonard, the Cook. You must obey her every direction."

"Go to the scullery, Gwen, and never come into the kitchen unless you're invited," said Mrs. Leonard, to titters from the other maids present, so that Gwen wondered if Mrs. Leonard was telling some sort of joke.

Gwen meekly followed Peggy, a girl perhaps a year or two older than she. Peggy was kind but apart from that, the rest of the evening was unpleasant. She did not know anybody, and when she was called to help set the supper for the other servants, she was introduced to an older man in a pressed suit of clothes who only glanced at her before walking away to take his seat at the head of the table in the servants' hall. He seemed to be in charge of all the servants and they all spoke respectfully to him. When everybody was seated around the long table, he told them that there was news, very good news, and they all fell silent.

"Mr. Saint-Saens will be arriving on Thursday next. He will be accompanied by his little daughter, Miss

Marie Louise Victoire. Mrs. Higgins, I hope the study and library are ready to receive him."

"Of course, they are," said the housekeeper smoothly.

"And the nursery—is it ready also?"

"Yes, Mr. Johnson." Mrs. Higgins barely held her peace.

"Capital, capital! And the nursery staff?"

"Mr. Johnson, Madam has said that the nursery staff are coming from France."

"That will be trouble," said Mr. Johnson with gloom. "They will complain, especially about the English food. They will send everything back down."

"Oh dear ... I will not do escargots," said Mrs. Leonard, pronouncing the 't' and 's'.

"*Escargoes,*" corrected Mr. Johnson.

The conversation went on, and nobody took any notice of Gwen, and she was relieved. The meat pie and soup were tasty, and there was as much bread and butter as she wanted. Apple tart followed. She ate her fill, and afterward she and Peggy washed, dried and put away the servants' dishes in the scullery.

CHAPTER FORTY

"Where are you from, Gwen?" asked Peggy that night when they were in their room getting ready for bed. Peggy was the kitchen-maid, and Madge was an under-housemaid. All spent most of their day below stairs.

Gwen hesitated before she said, "Saltwick Island."

"Saltwick Island? Where's that?"

As Gwen explained, the girls listened intently, and she realised that since they had never heard of Saltwick, they had no idea that *Saltwickers* were looked down upon. Instead, they seemed impressed.

"My cousin read me out a book about pirates that

took over an island, looking for gold," said Peggy. "Is there treasure on Saltwick?"

"Are there pirates?" Madge put in quickly.

Gwen giggled. "Once, I found a music-box on the mudflats. And my neighbours, they are incredibly lucky at finding things. As to pirates, there was a pirate who came to the island once, but the Ki—the Council—that's the men who are in charge—didn't like the look of him and they ran him off."

"Ran him off!" the girls said together, thrilled.

"That was brave of them!" said Madge.

"He could've come back with a ship full of pirates!" this from Peggy.

Then, another thought struck Madge, and she asked Gwen if she had ever been on the river in a boat. Her reply that she had made more trips in a boat than she could count amazed them, and furthermore, that she could row as good as any boy, caused Madge to say, "You lucky, lucky girl. I'd love to live on an island. Wouldn't you, Peggy?"

"Yes, I would. Oh la, I was so interested in Saltwick, that I got into bed and never noticed how cold it was, for once! And I clean forgot my prayers too! We can all say our prayers in bed tonight. Blow out the candle, Madge. Goodnight, girls."

Gwen buried herself under the blankets, prayed the Lord's Prayer, thought longingly of Nuru and Andy and her life on Saltwick, but then fell asleep until Madge woke her before dawn.

CHAPTER FORTY-ONE

"How was your afternoon off, Babs?" Mrs. Westingham asked with eagerness as she sat ready by her dressing-table.

Babs knew what her mistress wished to know.

"Why, Ma'am, I went to see Patricia, who knows the parlour maid at Rockwell. The family's arrived, they 'ave. The widower and the small child, a little girl, so, so pretty with big brown eyes! They are all taken with her."

"And—what's Mr. Saint-Saens like?"

"He's very handsome, Ma'am! If I was you, I would call on him without delay."

"That's enough, Babs," said Mrs. Westingham with sharpness.

"Very sorry, Ma'am," said Babs, in a little huff. She knew that her mistress wanted to marry Mr. Saint-Saens. She wanted to be rich again. It was a matter of great interest to everybody downstairs as to whether she would bag him or not. Babs closed her mouth firmly. She would give no more information until her mistress begged. She silently brushed her hair, counting three grey hairs and wondering if she would mention them tonight or keep it for another occasion.

"Who keeps house for our new neighbour?" asked Mrs. Westingham in a cold voice.

"His mother, I believe, Ma'am." Babs was still out of sorts and kept the information that his mother had a different name than her son, to herself.

Mrs. Westingham was pleased to hear that his mother was in residence. It would be quite proper for her to call and welcome her to the neighbourhood.

CHAPTER FORTY-TWO

Early one afternoon the following week, Mr. Saint-Saens and his mother were sitting in the drawing room. She was stitching a tapestry and he read the newspaper. The sound of the door knocker echoed through the house, and within a few moments Mr. Johnson came in with a card on a tray, handing it to Mrs. Brown.

"It must be for you, Madam. But they are evidently not aware that you have a different name than your son."

"Addressed to *Mrs. Saint-Saens*," she said with amusement. "A Mrs. Westingham paying us a call."

Jack looked up from the paper suddenly at the name Westingham. It was a name forever burned in bitterness in his memory from the letter Robert had sent him after Miss Compton had married. Could it be—could it be—surely not! She would not dare!

"Probably a near neighbour. I should like to meet her. Show her up, Johnson."

Mr. Johnson nodded and left the room, and Jack started up from his chair.

"Jack? Where are you going?"

"Mother, do you not remember—I knew her at one time—if it is the same lady. *Miss Jane Compton*." He blushed in confusion as he wrenched open the door.

"Oh, yes, of course." Mrs. Brown said. "I had quite forgotten that she married a Westingham! Off you go. There is no call for you to be here."

CHAPTER FORTY-THREE

J ane saw the little woman rise from her chair to greet her and stared in amazement. This was the tiresome old lady—Jack's mother—Mrs. Brown! What was she doing here?

"I'm sorry, there must be some misunderstanding," she began. "I was expecting a Mrs. Saint-Saens. But I'm acquainted with you. You are Mrs. Brown, the woman we used to know many years ago. I and my mother met you at Mrs. Fleetwood's in Grosvenor Square. Are you companion to Mrs. Saint-Saens, perhaps?"

"Indeed, I am Mrs. Brown, and I live here now. I am not a companion, though. I'm mistress of this house.

You may not be acquainted with the fact that my son is now Mr. Saint-Saens."

Jane looked about, bewildered.

"How can that be? And—which son?" she blurted out.

"Why, Jack, of course. You did not hear of his marriage?"

Jane was silenced. How was it that the poor tutor she had rejected became able to afford this splendid house and park? The truth came to her. He had married *money*. Married into an old, aristocratic family. She felt admiring of him and jealous at the same time. *Who were these Saint-Saens?* In her society days, she had never heard of them!

"Jack! Jack Brown!" burst out from her at last, as if she still could not believe it.

"It's a long story, but suffice it to say, he is no longer Mr. Brown. Please be seated, Mrs. Westingham. It's a long time since we met. How are you?"

Jane seemed to have gone a deathly white as she sat down in a satin-covered chair.

"Are you unwell, Mrs. Westingham? Some wine, perhaps?"

"Well, this is a surprise!" she gulped as she downed the ruby liquid a few minutes later.

"A great surprise, is it not?" Mrs. Brown smiled faintly as the memories of this attachment returned to her. She remembered why Miss Compton would not countenance a marriage with her son. He was not good enough for her, and she only a shopkeeper's daughter. Robert had told her that she had given Jack a great deal of encouragement—indeed, she had seen it with her own eyes when they had been in company together—and then had refused him. Jack had been so distraught that he had left London immediately.

"Mr Saint-Saens has a little daughter, I believe," said Mrs. Westingham pleasantly. "I should so like to see her. I'm sure she is the prettiest little thing imaginable. Pray what is her name?"

"She is Marie Louise Victoire."

"French names are so fashionable now." gushed Mrs. Westingham.

"She is French. Her mother was French."

"I should so like to see her." Mrs. Westingham repeated. "I have a little boy, Walter Daniel. He has just lost a tooth!" She had learned this in a letter received only that morning, written dutifully by the little boy himself, no doubt under the direction of his holier-than-thou Aunt Stella, who made him write once a week.

But Mrs. Brown was unmoved. "Marie Louise takes a nap at this time."

Mrs Westingham gave up her quest.

"Your little boy is at school, perhaps?" asked Mrs. Brown.

"I was widowed a short time ago," was Mrs. Westingham's plaintive answer. "My husband's affairs were in some confusion, and my son lives with his uncle for the present."

Mrs. Brown sympathised with Mrs. Westingham upon her loss and added that she hoped she would have her son back with her soon. What a comfort children were, when the other parent passed away! She had been widowed young also and would not have been able to keep going without her children.

"How is—Mr. Saint-Saens?" Jane asked after an appropriate pause had elapsed since this little speech.

"He is very well, thank you. He is not at home."

Jane's eyes wandered to the newspaper carelessly discarded on the table, the chair hastily pulled out.

There was a little more conversation and Jane got up to go. Mrs. Brown should return the call, but would she?

She took her leave gracefully. She was on foot, and on her way to the gate, she turned suddenly around, just in time to see a figure hastily conceal himself behind a curtain on a first-floor window. She smiled to herself in a little triumph. Not at home indeed! He still cared at least enough to be curious about how she looked, and if he did not, she would make him.

In the house, Jack hotly berated himself. What had possessed him to look out the landing window at Jane's departing back? And why had she looked around? He had been seen. She had caught him watching her. He returned to the drawing room, where his mother told him of the visit, the great surprise it had been to Mrs. Westingham to find her rejected suitor the master of this house. She had not hidden her amazement. Mr. Westingham had died recently. She was a widow.

Jack was only half-interested and rather cross. He asked his mother not to return the call to Mrs.

Westingham. A widow, was she? It made no difference.

CHAPTER FORTY-FOUR

S he would have to make the first move, Jane knew. To demonstrate her sincerity, she would have to humble herself. Should she write? No. A letter would not have the force of a face-to-face meeting, no matter what she wrote. A letter could be kept for later, if necessary, if he was reluctant to speak with her.

She lay awake thinking of her plan. How best to intercept him?

Where did the family go to church? Probably Christchurch, the nearest. She had not been to church for years, but she could bear a service or two if it reaped rewards for her.

The following Sunday morning, she got up early, donned her best hat and cloak and set off. A gracious carriage was outside the church! Was it that of Saint-Saens? The livery was very grand. Inside the church, she espied two footmen of the same livery. Seeing the carriage and the footmen deepened her desire to become the next Mrs. Saint-Saens.

All she had to do was to make him fall in love with her again.

She entered a pew halfway up. She disliked being in church, and the large sign near the altar 'GOD FORGIVES' was torture to her, even though she knew why she dragged her ball and chain about with her everywhere. She remembered Gwendoline's eyes —that last glimpse. She did not want to remember that! And her callousness toward her dying husband —he had deserved it!

She left again, determined to await him by his carriage, but if his mother was with him, much would be lost.

She saw him emerge and her heart fluttered. His hat had not been replaced upon his head, and she had a good view of him. He had not lost his looks. He was handsome as ever, the errant lock falling over his forehead. He pushed it back and looked around, greeted some people with smiles, and was being introduced to others by the rector.

There was no sign of his mother. Excellent!

He saw her as he approached his carriage a few minutes later. His step slowed, he looked to one side, his face flushed.

"Jack," she said softly, approaching him to be out of hearing of the footmen and coachman who were nearby. "Jack, do you not know me? Please look at me! Oh, I see you blame me! I, who was only embarrassed and ashamed at what I—we—had done, who sent you away! How I have regretted it every day of my life since then!" She dropped her head and covered her forehead with her hand.

He glanced briefly at her, his fascinating eyes cold, and strode past her, getting into his carriage without a word. "Walk on!" she heard his coachman say, and the horses moved off.

CHAPTER FORTY-FIVE

J ack mused on the unexpected encounter on the way home in the carriage. It had affected him greatly, and it could even be said to have disturbed him.

Miss Compton—no, Mrs. Westingham—he corrected himself—had hardly altered. Perhaps she looked a little older, but she retained her beauty. Her complexion was luminous, and he had espied waves of golden hair under her hat. Her wide-set blue eyes held an appeal that had shaken him. Why was he so affected by her? What was it that she had said? He recalled the words.

I, who was only embarrassed and ashamed at what I had done, who sent you away! How I have regretted it every day of my life since then!

Embarrassed and ashamed ... sent you away ... the words replayed themselves in his mind for the rest of the day, even when he and the nurse took Marie Louise for a walk.

Is that what had happened? Could he believe her? She had said very cruel things—about his station in life, his prospects, even about his nature. He remembered how used he had felt.

Marie Louise chatted and babbled by his side. It troubled him often to see his little daughter without a mother. Nurses were all very well, but they came and went, and could not possibly have the same love and interest a mother had. The two who had arrived from France were returning home soon and were only waiting to allow two more to be engaged to take their places.

He wanted the best for his daughter. His only child.

He thought he might marry again, sometime. As much as for his own companionship as for Marie Louise to have a mother. He would have to choose carefully, for her sake. Again, Mrs. Westingham drifted into his head. He remembered his deep feelings for her, his crushing heartbreak when she had dismissed him forever. Those feelings were barely under the surface, and it angered him that they had not died. They were a sleeping volcano. He found that he did not trust them.

CHAPTER FORTY-SIX

Gwen settled in with the help of the other young maids and was surprised to find herself content in Rockwell. The situation of the house and parklands pleased her, and on her afternoons off she put on a cloak and went down to the Thames and walked along a path near the river, enjoying its sights and sounds. She always imagined the river flowing upon its winding journey as far as Essex, where it met the sea. If she had a boat and was so inclined, she could row herself home. But there was no need for that—she was fed and content and had friends. How had this contentment stolen upon her, unawares? She missed Andy and Nuru, and thought of them on Sundays when at church, and before she fell asleep at night. But though her work was tiring, with days of scouring tables, and scrubbing floors on her hands and knees; of carrying heavy buckets and hauling coal here and there, she slept very well.

She, Peggy and Madge became true friends and they had many laughs together and helped each other out, covering for each other so that nobody got into trouble. The girls had come from workhouses and they had stories in common. Peggy had never known her mother, and Madge had only a vague memory of hers. Gwen did not tell them about what her mother had tried to do to her. She realised that to most people, it was something unbelievable. A mother who hated her child was a rarity. Gwen pondered it sometimes by the river, and she was glad to be too busy at other times to allow it to disturb her. Nuru Paul was her mother, and before that, Aunt Ellen. The other woman was a stranger.

She used to think that she was bad and that was why that terrible thing had happened. A little older now, she saw clearly where the wickedness lay, and it was not with her. She hoped she would never have to meet the woman who had been her 'real mother' again.

Gwen was not at all confined to the scullery; that had been Mrs. Leonard's little joke. Mrs. Higgins was not as strict as she had thought; some days she was in a light-hearted mood and teased the surly Mr. Johnson, and if she was in a bad mood you only had to admire her brooch and she was right as rain again. Mrs. Higgins loved brooches and had a marvellous selection with which she pinned her little everyday puce or violet shawl. Whenever her brooch was admired, she would pat it as if it were a little pet carried on her bosom, and smile, and tell you how it came to be hers and when. Little Marie Louise loved the housekeeper; her glittering brooch brought smiles as she demanded to be lifted up the better to see it.

The upper housemaids were a little stand-offish, but Gwen did not have much to do with them anyway. The male employees, footmen mostly, were good fun and flirted constantly with Peggy, who was very pretty and pert with them.

The only footman who took any notice of Gwen was Jeremy Markham. She noticed that he was not very popular with the other footmen, and the maids gave him a wide berth. Madge said it was because he carried tales and exaggerated to make himself somebody. His family were all upper servants in great houses, he claimed, and he was only biding his time here, though he liked the livery very much, it being very ornate.

Markham had a knack for gathering information, and every night he held forth in the Servants' Hall, telling stories that many took with a grain of salt. Mr. Johnson, Mrs. Higgins, Mrs. Leonard and Mrs. Brown's maid, Perkins, were never present for these sessions, and there was nobody to check his flow of conversation. One evening he claimed that the Mistress was afraid to wear the colour green because it was supposed to be unlucky. This was disputed by Nancy, a parlourmaid.

"Have you ever seen her wear green, then?" persisted Markham, who was repairing a chipped china vase with a little cement on the point of a knife.

"No," Nancy admitted.

"Have any of you ever seen the Mistress of this house wear green?" he asked, looking around at the maids while they mended linen and carried out other chores that could be done in the evenings while they were sitting around. Mrs. Higgins did not allow them to be idle.

They all had to admit that they had never seen Mrs. Brown in green.

"There!" he said with triumph. "It's unlucky, that's why! And do you know why it's thought unlucky? Because green dye contains arsenic, that's why."

He told them snippets of news from the dining room and from all over the house. A dinner guest had said that the Government would fall soon, and that he had it straight from Westminster. The Bank of England was going to be in serious trouble before summer. And there was more personal information —the Mistress's memory was going. Perkins was in fear of her life that her Mistress would misplace something valuable and she'd be accused of stealing it. And Mr. Saint-Saens was going to an auction to buy paintings for the gallery, where by rights there should be paintings of the Family, only there were not enough of them to fill the space, so he was thinking of Constable's, but Mrs. Brown wanted portraits of past Kings and Queens and the Duke of Wellington, whom she deeply admired. He was very fond of paintings, was the master.

"Constables!" said Mable, the housemaid, looking around with a sort of hilarious disbelief.

"I refer to John Constable, the famous painter," Markham informed her with pomposity.

"How do you know about him, Markham?" Peggy interjected.

"Everybody knows John Constable," he snorted.

There was a silence. He had a way of making everybody feel inferior. He could read and write very well and told everybody that he would be a butler someday. How he would make sure the silver was polished to within an inch of its life! Mr. Johnson was not as particular as he should be, about silver.

One evening he announced that he had delivered a letter to the Master, and that it was in a lady's hand. Mr. Saint-Saens had not been very pleased to see it.

"Of course, he's a very desirable catch for any rich young woman." Markham continued. "And I'll wager it was a letter from one of them. He's probably plagued with women."

Madge snorted.

"No woman would write a letter to a man unasked. What do you think was in it, Markham? *Dear Sir, I'd love to marry you. Do ask me!?*

Everybody chuckled at this, and Markham looked rather cross.

Gwen had not heard the exchange, as she was at the end of the table, too absorbed in her needlework, and her mind had drifted. So, she did not laugh. This caught the attention of Mr. Markham, and he thought that she did not share the mirth of the others at his expense. Of all the servants, he concluded that Gwendoline was the only one who had anything in common with him, and he would therefore give her the reward of his attention from now on. After that, he placed himself near her, and went out of his way to speak to her, to deliberately deprive the others of his superior knowledge and to give her the benefit of all he had learned upstairs.

CHAPTER FORTY-SEVEN

"He likes you, Jer Markham does." Peggy said, getting up from her knees after saying her night prayers.

"Oh no, he sits near me to annoy you all." Gwen had realised this, as she had often seen Markham look about in dissatisfaction at the others around the table, after he had said something he thought was very important. He said things loudly, hoping to catch the others' interest.

"Don't encourage 'im," Madge said, scrubbing her face with a towel.

"I don't. I hope it doesn't look as if I am," Gwen said. "He talks on and on and I don't even look at him, do I? I'm afraid I'll make a mistake in my work. I hope people don't think I like him."

"No, don't worry. We just thought we'd warn you," Peggy said, jumping into bed. "Oh, this is cold!"

"You say that every night, Peggy Watkins, why don't you fill a warming-pan, if you're so cold?" Madge asked.

"I'm too lazy. And I get over it in a minute. Blow out the candle, Madge. G'night."

Gwen lay awake for a little while. Jeremy Markham was a bit of a nuisance, but she did not know how to shake him off. She never idled with him in the hallways, and never spoke first to him, unless she had to. She hoped that Jeremy did not think she liked him.

Her mind drifted to Saltwick, as it always did before she went to sleep, to the tough little plants on the cliffs, the grasses waving in the wind, the mudflats, the beach, the fields of willow. Who lived in their cabin now? Were they tending their garden? How was Betty, and Mrs. White? The Marcus family, the Gibsons, Fosters, Kwamis, McDonnells and others? How could she ever get news of them? She could not write well enough to compose a letter and felt a little wary of asking somebody to do so for her. Especially Jeremy Markham.

Besides, she was very private about Saltwick. For some reason, Mrs. Higgins thought she came from the Isle of Wight, and that's what everybody thought now. It was just as well, for Gwen had absorbed the islanders' reticence to speak of Saltwick when she was in 'the World.' Perhaps even Peggy and Madge had forgotten.

She was quite happy that everybody thought she was from the Isle of Wight, wherever that was.

CHAPTER FORTY-EIGHT

Mr. Saint-Saens re-read the letter. It was a plea from the heart, explaining and expanding on that topic that had been raised outside the church only two weeks ago. The writing was blotched and streaked, as if with tears, with apologies and self-recrimination.

He paced up and down the library. He had to answer it but had delayed for as long as was possible without giving grave offense. He finally took his pen and paper and began to write. As he did, a warm rush of feelings spread over him.

It would have been so easy for Jane to have placed the blame for their tryst on him, but she had not done so—had never implied that their sin had been his fault, his instigation, or that he had forced her in any way, as his brother Robert had feared she would do, causing his hasty departure from London. She did not refer to that at all, only apologised for offending him by seeing him off so rudely after he had offered his hand. It was a humble letter, and she finished it by saying that she did not deserve any attention from him.

He wanted to see her, and the more he thought of it, the deeper his feelings. The volcano was flaming again, and he was swamped with love. He could hardly wait to meet her, to be with her again!

But his head warned him into some caution. So, when he wrote his answer, he invited her to dinner with him and his mother next Saturday evening. It would be a quiet affair with little opportunity for any emotion or intimacy. He wished to observe her. There were other questions—like why her son was not living with her. In her letter, she had hinted at a conspiracy against her from her husband's family and how she had been misjudged, and the blotchiest part of the letter was when she had written of how she missed her darling little boy, and the injustice of the world against a lone, helpless widow.

CHAPTER FORTY-NINE

Saturday arrived and the Saint-Saens carriage was sent to convey Mrs. Westingham to Rockwell. Mrs. Brown, who had only been informed that day of the visit and had given her son a piece of her mind at not warning her, dressed less elegantly than expected for guests, to show her visitor that she was not welcomed by her. It galled her to see Jack paying this woman any attention, and she made up her mind to write to Robert to get him to come and put a stop to it.

Dinner passed pleasantly enough, with general conversation, and they retired to the drawing room together, as there was no man to keep Jack company over his port. There, Jane launched into an outpouring of her troubles as if Mrs. Brown was not there. She regarded Jack's mother as a dull, boring woman who was not worthy of regard. And it was obvious she was a little senile—she had twice called the footman to enquire about sauce for the chicken, and it was there in front of her.

"You must wonder why my son is in the guardianship of his uncle, rather than being left with his mother. His uncle always disliked me; yes, he and his wife, from the first, set out to make my life difficult. He set my own husband against me. They have everything to their advantage—the best lawyers, connections in high places that I cannot match. In every dispute, they win."

Jane expected to be shown the child, but there was no suggestion of meeting Marie Louise, and after a discreet yawn from the old woman around eight-thirty, she knew she should be taking her leave. She did so, managing a look of longing toward Jack when the old woman's back was turned.

"Please call upon me," she whispered. "I am so alone now! But I'm not in any position to return the compliment of a dinner such as you have provided for me this evening."

Jack's heart was touched. While the carriage was taking her home, he poured himself another port and wondered why she had such an effect upon him.

All through dinner, he could hardly take his eyes from her. She was beautiful—and sad. The room had seemed empty when she had left. The resentment he had felt for her had faded. She'd been young. She was repentant. She was suffering.

CHAPTER FIFTY

M rs. Brown never wrote to her older son telling him of Jack's reunion with the woman who had rejected him. She forgot. Jack's infatuation went unchecked except for his own caution, and it was fortunate that he had learned to be cautious.

He called to see Mrs. Westingham the following week, and as they sat in her little parlour together, she wept on his shoulder. She had sent her servant out, and though he had tender feelings for her, he knew what would happen if they fell into the same situation as before. This time it would be his honourable nature, not an impetuous love, that would make him propose marriage. Though he knew he loved her, he was not ready to trust her. It was far too soon. He extricated himself and put a distance between them.

"If you wish to show me any legal papers about the Guardianship, I can take a look. With your permission, I could entrust them to my lawyers. I have the best, quite as good as, or better than your in-laws."

"That is very kind of you—" Jane bit her lip. "—but I cannot afford your lawyers."

She was a little offended at his removing himself from her. She thought it would be easy.

"Oh, Jane. Please do not think about the expense. I want you to be happy, and I know your greatest happiness would be found in your child being returned to you. I am a parent too, and fathers can love quite as deeply as mothers."

What a fool, Jane thought to herself. Aloud, she said: "There is no point in pursuing it, Jack, when I don't have the means of providing for him."

He was silent. He knew what was in the air. It irritated him that she expected him to renew his advances, that she assumed that he was so besotted with her that he would sweep every objection aside.

"Jack. You do not know this. I looked for you, to

apologise for my rudeness, all those years ago. But you had left London very quickly, and I had no way to find you!"

"What is that?" he spun around.

She repeated herself, adding: "If you had not left so suddenly, we might have patched it all up very quickly. Now so many years have gone by, and there is little hope of us living our lives together."

Jane was thinking quickly.

"I do not ask to be your wife," she said plainly. "I am far below you now. Not your wife, but—"

He looked at her, astonished.

"A court would never return your son to you if you were my mistress," he said.

She looked at him, her long-lashed eyes wide.

"Perhaps he is better off where he is. He has every opportunity that I cannot give him. He has cousins who are like brothers and sisters to him. He regards his uncle as his father. Perhaps I am being selfish in wanting to take him away from where he has settled in happiness." She turned away and looked out the window.

"Jane, I will never take a mistress. It's against my principles."

"Your principles are high, and I admire them greatly. I wish I had been raised with principles. My mother allowed me to do as I pleased, and my father never had a kind word for me."

Jane broke into fresh tears and flung herself on the sofa.

"I was wrong to offer myself as your mistress. I just love you—why do I have to keep it secret? Why can't I say it, loud and clear? I love you, Jack Brown."

He softened but did not approach.

"Jane. It's too soon for such talk. I'm only just out of mourning, and I have a little child whose future I must carefully consider. I may never marry again, or then again, I may. I don't know. But I must go now. It's time for Marie Louise to have her afternoon walk, and I always accompany her. You must meet Marie Louise," he said, impulsively.

"Meet her? You would allow me to meet her?" she sat up, her cheeks streaked with tears, her eyes full of hope.

"Yes. Shall we all take a walk together, this day next

week, at this time? I shall take the carriage and call for you. We shall go to Kensington Gardens."

It was better than nothing, and she agreed. Jack put on his hat and bid her adieu, and she was left in her parlour, trying to make sense of him.

When he had asked her to walk with him, she had been happy—very happy to perhaps be shown the fine gardens and shrubberies of Rockwell, and the interior of the house perhaps. It might have meant that he was considering her to be mistress of it all sometime, even though he seemed unsure. He still had feelings for her. But no, marriage was not to be. At least not yet.

She knew she would never allow him to see the Guardianship papers. There was so much written about her in those pages, and all of it was true.

CHAPTER FIFTY-ONE

"You wished to see me, sir?" Mrs. Higgins entered the study and before her eyes met that of her employer, they took in the disorder of the room. Books strewn about everywhere, several open, on top of others. Pens, inks, sheaves of paper, some blank, many scrawled upon.

"I see you disapprove of the disorder in my little hideaway from the world," he smiled, taking a seat behind his desk. "My mother does not dare to set foot in here. Actually, it is of my mother that I wish to speak, Mrs. Higgins. Please have a seat."

She pulled out a chair, taking a book from it and setting it rather pointedly upon the desk.

"Oh, I am sorry. So few persons come to me here. I

wished to see you in my study rather than in the drawing room, because my mother could interrupt us. Mrs. Higgins, perhaps you've noticed that my mother's memory is not as good as it was."

"Yes, sir, I have noticed that. She gives orders for the kitchen that are frequently for the wrong day, for instance, thinking Saturday is Sunday, or Sunday is Monday. Cook and I adjust it accordingly, and she does not seem to remember, at dinner time, that she ordered something different that very morning. I hope we do right, sir?"

"Of course, you do. Mrs. Higgins. It seems you're very much aware of the challenges she presents then. I think, Mrs. Higgins, that you will have to be mistress of this house, without allowing my mother to know it, if you know what I mean? Even to the point of managing the nursery."

"Of course, sir. I felt it would come to that. Her memory is not something that's likely to get better, unfortunately. I have developed the habit of visiting the nursery daily. Miss Marie Louise and I have become the best of friends by now."

"She speaks of *Miss Higgs*, yes! As for my mother's memory, you are correct—I am afraid it will only get worse."

"And in the absence of anybody you can call upon to be mistress of the house, I would be happy to act, sir, and as you say, discreetly. Without hurting your mother's feelings. May I ask, sir, if she is herself aware of this problem?"

Mrs. Higgins knew the answer to this. Mrs. Brown's lady's maid confided in her, but she wanted the Master's opinion.

"She must know but is unwilling to admit it, at least as yet. Thank you for your help, Mrs. Higgins. If I might confide something else—you know of the visits here of a lady named Mrs. Westingham, and perhaps the staff have possibly concluded that there will be another mistress—"

"Sir, I would not and have never presumed—"

"It's quite all right. I just want to tell you that it is not likely to happen, at least not for the foreseeable future, so you can put a stop to any gossip downstairs …"

"I am glad you mentioned it, sir. I will do as you ask. Sir, do you think that I might allow a maid in here to dust and beat the carpets?" She cast her eyes about again.

He laughed at her obviously disapproving eye.

"Mrs. Higgins, I understand your inclination. She may, but with strict instructions not to turn any pages over or disturb the order of any books I have laid open. There is a method to my work."

"Work, sir?"

"Yes, of course, work! Do you not know, Mrs. Higgins, that I always earned my living? You must know I was a lowly tutor at one time! I can't abide being idle! All this—" he swept his arm about "is my plan to educate the children of the poor. I'm writing text-books and will, I hope, begin a school someday, perhaps even in this house—but there is much to be done first, with regard to my affairs in France, and various other legal matters. I have engaged an assistant, and soon you will see a new man about the house, name of Fleming. He's the son of a former neighbour of mine. A good young man, very keen to improve himself, and shares my passion for education."

"I'm relieved you informed me, sir, about the new stranger about the house! And I had no idea about the school! That I admire! I must say, sir, that when I first took up this situation, I wondered at the calibre of the persons you were meaning to employ downstairs. But the maids are a group of hardworking, good girls, and I have no complaint to make about their work or their characters."

"That's good to know, Mrs. Higgins. Have I converted you, then?" he smiled.

"How did you know I needed converting, Mr. Saint-Saens?"

"My mother told me you were a little sceptical."

"Yes, I was, but a little thinking on my part, because of my own personal misfortune, brought me around —you see—" his interested expression gave her leave to expand, so she told him about her family's misfortune. He had not known.

"That's why you are so fond of fine jewellery, then." he said, his eyes flicking to today's brooch, a gold seed-pearl clasp, which she instinctively patted before she could stop herself, giving him a little smile. He had the grace to look away as she blushed.

"If that is all, sir, I must be going back to my duties," she said, getting up and pushing in the chair.

"Yes of course. I'm sorry to have delayed you." he said, in a bit of a rush. He was a little red now.

"Not at all sir, you are not to think of it." She rushed

from the room. She stopped and took a deep breath outside the door.

Leonora, control yourself. There is no hope, not a shred!

But it pleased her greatly that her taste in superior ornaments had been noticed by her employer! And —now that she was mistress of the house, at least in practice if not in name, she would have to consult him often about staffing and other matters. Of course, she must be very formal and if she had any feelings, hide them. Today had been an aberration— an unexpected departure from formality because—*of what?* She did not wish to pursue her thoughts, but she was in good humour for the rest of the evening, teased Mr. Johnson at dinner, and the staff decided that Mr. Saint-Saens had raised her wages.

CHAPTER FIFTY-TWO

Gwen was in the kitchen garden, her very favourite spot apart from the riverside, when a strange young man entered through the little wooden gate and looked about in bewilderment.

"Are you lost, sir?" she asked him, straightening up from the bed of lemon basil.

"Er, yes." He looked about again.

"Are you a tradesman?"

"No actually," he strode toward her, took off his hat and bowed slightly, "I'm amanuensis to Mr. Saint-Saens, and I have never been in such a confusing place in my entire life. I declare I left his study only a short time ago to make my way out. I took one hallway, then another, and a stairway, and I left the house by a door somewhere near a cherry tree and a stone urn, and then a cat's head appeared suddenly over a shrub and stared at me with a very hostile air, and after that I wandered about, and now I don't know if I am still in Chelsea." He grinned.

He was a handsome, copper-haired man with brown eyes—a combination that Gwendoline found captivating. She had never seen anybody like him before.

"I should introduce myself, if I'm still on the Saint-Saens property," he went on. "William Fleming, at your service." He bowed his head.

Gwen was greatly surprised that anybody would speak with such civility to a maid. She was wearing her cap and her apron and that was streaked with earth. Her fingernails had earth underneath them.

"You're still on Saint-Saens property," she assured him, smiling. "I'm Gwendoline Paul. What did you say you were, to the master?"

"Amanuensis. It's a fancy name for a secretary or an assistant in work of a clerical nature."

"Oh! That makes sense. He needs an assistant. I had

to help the housemaids clean his study. You won't tell him what I said, will you?"

"I shall be silent. Don't look now, but there's a very severe-looking woman at an upstairs window looking down upon us. She may be related to the cat. The stare is the same."

Gwen giggled.

"Oh dear, that is surely Mrs. Higgins, the housekeeper. She'll think I have a follower!" Gwen blushed slightly; she would not mind a follower like Mr. Fleming!

"I shall save you from her fancy. Begin to point me in the right direction, fling your arms out this way and that, and she'll go away."

Gwen had to suppress her chuckles. She gave him directions to the front of the house, making the appropriate movements, even walking with him to the little wooden gate.

"She left the window. You are quite safe, but I didn't hear a word you said, as her scrutiny of me was unnerving. I should be terrified of such a supervisor. Could you repeat your directions?"

CHAPTER FIFTY-THREE

Before long, everybody knew who Mr. Fleming was and he was an accepted part of the household. He had a good influence on their master, because the study was in order. Mr. Fleming did not live in, he stayed in lodgings nearby.

Gwen tried her best to avoid Jeremy Markham, not because she had taken a fancy to Mr. Fleming (though she admired him, he was far above her) but to avoid giving the second footman the wrong impression. But it was nearly impossible. He continuously sought her out to tell her things, most of which she did not want to know. His crowing of knowing more than he should, of hearing when nobody thought he was listening, of lingering at doors, was irritating.

Mr. Fleming always used the tradesmen's entrance, and when their paths crossed in the long back hallway—the long way around to Mr. Saint-Saens's study—he was always on for banter with any of the maids he met. Gwen did not think that he favoured her in particular, though she had allowed herself to dream of him for a little while. His brown eyes had a perpetual twinkle.

But Gwen's heart was still on Saltwick Island. She should have returned long ago, but saving was harder than she thought. Her quarterly payments of two pounds and ten shillings seemed to disappear. Peggy and Madge loved a little style, and bargain-hunted whenever they were in the village. When she was with either girl she bought trinkets and ribbons, too. And when she had been paid last week, she'd bought a hat—a real hat—for Sundays. Peggy and Madge had urged her on. It was a little creation in white, with green and yellow silk flowers about the brim, and long green ribbons down the back. The first Sunday she wore it she felt like a lady and hoped that Mr. Fleming admired her in it. Mrs. Higgins looked a little disapprovingly at her but said nothing. Maids were not supposed to dress above their station.

She knew that she could not return to Saltwick soon

if she kept on spending as she was doing. But it was so difficult to resist pretty things, and Chelsea was full of shops! And they got leave to go to a Fair, which with its games and entertainments, gobbled up money like nothing else on earth.

CHAPTER FIFTY-FOUR

CHELSEA

TWO YEARS LATER

"There's a visitor expected next week," Markham told Gwen one day. "His name is Barrett-Smith, and the master made his acquaintance on board ship on the way home from France. I expect he'll be disappointed there's no hunt or shoots or anything of that nature. Our master, Gwen, is a very dull fellow compared to the place where my brother Fred is at. His master is always out hunting and fishing and horse-racing."

"I don't think the master is as dull as you say," Gwen mused, halting her knitting for a moment. "He writes tracts and books and wants all his staff to read and write. Mrs. Higgins told me I am to learn!"

She had seen Mr. Saint-Saens many times in the distance, peering at him when he was out of doors with Marie Louise and she was in the kitchen garden gathering herbs or in the flower garden choosing flowers for the still room. Cook told her that she was good at selecting just the right flavourings for the pot, and Mrs. Higgins told her that she showed promise in working with aromatic plants and herbs. The housekeeper spent a great deal of time in the still room, the last room on the long hallway, and the largest. There she made medicinal cordials and fragrant oils and there, also, was where the fruit was prepared for jam-making. A fire burned to keep the room warm for drying flowers, and to Gwen the room smelled like a summer day on Saltwick, with fragrances filling the air.

She was thrilled to hear the housekeeper's praise and lapped up all the information she could. Mrs. Higgins was pleasantly surprised at her interest and one day allowed her to help in the making of lavender oil, using the still. It was complicated and she had to watch it carefully, but she was very pleased with the result, which Mrs. Higgins gathered into a dark little bottle for Mrs. Brown.

This would be a good skill for when she returned home, for oils and perfumes would sell in Rush. She wondered how much a still cost. It was nothing at all like the still that the men of Saltwick made whiskey with. She'd seen that once when Betty had taken her to the back window of a shed attached to the McDonnells' cottage, and she'd peered in at the barrel, pipe and urn, and she had been mystified as to why they were a secret. Betty told her that she must not say that she had seen it, for she would get into trouble with her parents. Betty also told her about the room under the floor for hiding the still when the police were seen on the water.

Mrs. Higgins's still was a polished copper pot and a spotless glass tube going into a glass bowl, with a little vial at the end of the tube to catch the oil. There were books in the still room about drying and distilling herbs and flowers. She wished she could read better, for she wanted to try everything!

"Reading? I don't believe you. You heard wrong," said Markham flatly, annoyed in case it was true about everybody learning to read and write.

"No, I've been told by Mrs. Higgins," she replied firmly. "We're to use the schoolroom upstairs. Me, and the carpenter's children, and the stable boys, and the new scullery maid. I'll go on my afternoon off, every Wednesday at three o'clock."

"You're a girl, you don't need education."

"How am I to know how to make oils and soaps, if I can't read the receipts? And I need to know how to keep an account-book, too."

Markham was stupefied into silence. After a few minutes, he said, "The master is going on a picnic next Sunday. I'm to go."

"Oh, lucky you! Where to?"

"Holland Park. All the footmen are going, but no maids, except Perkins of course, to help Mrs. Brown. And the nursery maids."

"Oh, for shame, that none of us can go."

"Cook is packing a large hamper. I'll tell you something else, but you must keep it to yourself, for these people—" he indicated the rest of the staff seated about the table— "gossip a lot. He's taking Mrs. Westingham out again."

"Who is Mrs. Westingham?"

"A widow. Mr. Saint-Saens has taken a great liking to her. I wouldn't be the least bit surprised if they got married. But he hasn't been in any hurry. He's been keeping her on a string for the last two years. Have you never seen her, then?"

"Never. What's she like, this Mrs. Westingham?"

"Old, well over thirty. But that would be all right for him. He's older than that. She's a handsome woman, I have to say, for her age. She's been to dinner several times, and luncheon more times than I can count, and goes on outings with Master and Miss Marie Louise."

"If they did get married, what kind of mistress would she make?" mused Gwen.

Markham leaned in close to her ear.

"I would not like her. Not at all. No, not with what I hear tell of her. They say, that her husband, Mr. Daniel Westingham, *died in mysterious circumstances*. Now! What do you think of that?"

"That's shocking." Gwen cast off her knitting, a dishcloth made from twine.

"You say that, but you don't seem to be shocked by it really! I thought you'd jump out of your skin!"

Gwen was silent.

"I'm sure it's just gossip," she said, getting up. "I can't talk for longer, I have to check that the still room is clean." She took a candle and left the table. She always had to find an excuse to get away from Markham.

Gwen was disturbed by what she had heard but said nothing.

She knew that people like Mrs. Westingham existed; that is, if what Markham had said about her was true. It made her feel a little ill to think that her master might marry somebody whose husband died in *'mysterious circumstances,'* but there was nothing she could do about it.

CHAPTER FIFTY-FIVE

Sunday was a beautiful day for a picnic. While the family went to Holland Park, Mrs. Leonard made lemonade and the servants went outside to the apple orchard and had a small picnic of their own in the shade of a large tree.

After eating her sandwich and ice-cream, Gwen walked for a little way, then stretched out on the sunny grass and looked up at the sky. She was sure it was a beautiful day in Saltwick, just the kind of day that she and the other children used to spend all day out of doors. They clambered about on rocks and fished in pools and raced each other into the water. On those long sunny days, nobody had a care in the world. What was everybody doing this very minute on Saltwick? The old people were sitting in the shade, mothers were chatting together, fishermen enjoying the Saltwick brew, telling each other tall tales.

I wonder if Bob White and the other boys came back. I wonder how Betty is. She could be married by now, for she must be nearly twenty. I wonder if the King is still in charge. How many babies have been born since I left, and how many people have died? I hope there haven't been drownings. Have they many artists this year?

She drifted to sleep in the sun and dreamed that she had returned to Saltwick in a boat, and nobody there saw her. They were running about in chaos, fleeing somebody or something fearful. The boats were launched in a great hurry, babies and small children were handed in and their parents got in quickly after them and rowed away, leaving her standing on the stone beach.

"You can't go away! Can't you see I'm coming home?"

"What's the matter, Gwen?"

She opened her eyes to see Madge bending over her, blocking the sun.

"You were shouting. What's the matter?"

"I had a bad dream." Gwen sat up. Her head was splitting.

"She's had too much sun," scolded Cook from the shade of the tree. "You'd best go inside, girl. You should never fall asleep in the sun! Go upstairs and rest a while in the dark."

After an hour, she felt better and went downstairs again. The footmen were back from the picnic and were all agog about it. They had had a wonderful time.

On Sundays, there wasn't any work to be done after the washing up of the dinner plate from upstairs, so they sat around and talked. As usual, Markham placed himself beside Gwen.

"What I heard today was astonishing," he said, covering the side of his mouth with his hand. "I didn't mean to eavesdrop, but they think we don't have ears, you know. They forget we're there!"

He proceeded to tell Gwen what he had discovered, before she could put a stop to it.

CHAPTER FIFTY-SIX

Holland Park was full of picnic parties. A band played and everybody was in wonderful humour. The Saint-Saens party found a pretty spot within sight of a cultivated garden on one side, and a meadow of colourful wildflowers on the other. Markham and the other footmen had opened the hamper and laid out all the food on a tablecloth, then lingered nearby to attend the family if they needed anything while they ate their own food. They had been within easy earshot of the party.

The other two manservants were chatting together about the races, and Markham, who did not bet, was munching his ham sandwich and could easily overhear the conversation of the family a little way off. They had finished lunch, and Marie Louise was running about and got stung by something. The master had made a big fuss and held her for a time, after which he got down again on the grass and chatted with Mrs. Westingham. Then the nurses decided to take the child for a walk to the meadow, and Perkins encouraged Mrs. Brown to go also. So only Mrs. Westingham was left with the master.

He wondered if he should move away a bit—he did not want to hear any love-talk—that would be wrong, to eavesdrop on that—he'd move away if it started. He heard Mrs. Westingham speak.

"Jack, now that we are alone, there is something I simply must tell you. I have had it on my mind for so long, because I did not know if you would be very angry with me. I suppose you will be, though."

There was a pause, and Markham began to draw away a little, it wasn't love-talk, but it was private. Curiousity got the better of him, however.

"We—you and I—had a child." were her next words.

Markham became very still. He hardly dared to chew his sandwich.

"A child? What are you talking about?" his master said.

"A little girl was born to us, on the 5th of November 1856. Do you understand what I'm telling you?"

The master sat upright and turned to look at her with intensity.

"Jane, you are jesting with me. Stop."

CHAPTER FIFTY-SEVEN

"November 1856?" Gwen said incredulously. Surely it was just a coincident. She knew that she was born in 1856 on the 5th of November. Aunt Ellen used to bake a cake for her on Guy Fawkes Day because it was her birthday.

"Yes, Guy Fawkes Day. And so, they talked on, very angrily—she was not jesting, and Mr. Saint-Saens believed her. He wanted to know what was done with the baby, and Mrs. Westingham said she gave it to a woman who would find a family to adopt it."

"I'm sure none of it is true," Gwen said. She felt a trembling come over her.

"What's wrong, Gwen? You're shaking."

"I got too much sun today. I fell asleep in the sun."

"That's a bad thing to do. You shouldn't do that. You could get sunstroke and *freckles*."

"I think I'll go upstairs now."

She made her way up the back staircase, her heart thumping. She paused at the green baize door that led out into the main staircase, that of the house. Was Mrs. Westingham in this house now? Was the whole thing just a coincidence? Was it another woman, another baby? Surely it was so. She calmed herself down and fell into bed, still suffering the effects of the sun.

CHAPTER FIFTY-EIGHT

"Ho-ho, there's trouble, there is." Markham told her only a few days later. Gwen was busy in the still room topping and tailing gooseberries. Markham had come in under the pretext of looking for a missing knife. "I was sent around to Grace Street with a letter for Mrs. Westingham. It wasn't sealed properly. Gwen, I can trust you, can't I? We are as thick as thieves, aren't we? I don't mind your wearing spectacles."

Gwen managed a faint wry smile. *Odious*, she thought.

"I saw it." Markham went on.

"You mean—you read it?"

"I did."

"You shouldn't have done that."

"I know. Don't tell, will you? But—I wanted to know, because—I got an idea, but I'll tell you about it some other time. The master has ordered Mrs. W. to find out what happened to the child or else."

"Or else what?"

"Or else he won't ever see 'er again! Now what do you think of that?"

"It's very silly. The child could be anywhere. If that was '56, she's nearly grown by now!"

"She's out there somewhere though. The master, you see, wants her to have whatever is due to her as his daughter. I have to go now, but when I see you next, I might have more news."

"I wish you wouldn't open other peoples' letters," Gwen said a little sharply. She did not want to find out that Mrs. Westingham was her mother. What would she do, if she was sure? If she married and became Marie Louise's mother—would that little girl be in danger too? The very thought made her feel ill.

"Don't nag me, Gwen." Markham said, peremptorily leaving the room.

CHAPTER FIFTY-NINE

Jane Westingham wondered if she had had too much sun that day in Holland Park, or perhaps too much wine. *What had possessed her to confess to Jack?* All had been going very well! She hadn't intended to. But Gwendoline was on her mind, and had been of late, in spite of her drinking more than was good for her to blot her out. Her eyes rose before her, the blue-green eyes as she was dropping into the water, and she could not stand the memory.

Gwendoline was on her mind most probably because Jack had a daughter. Jack thought that Marie Louise was the most perfect little girl in the world. He gave her too much attention. At the picnic last Sunday, before they had lunch, Marie Louise had been stung on the hand by an insect. Instead of allowing the nurse to deal with it—the nurse who was paid handsomely for that very purpos—Jack had gotten to his feet and swung her up in his arms and made a fuss and kissed it better. He sat down on the grass again and, with his arm about his daughter, he talked with Jane, and Marie Louise gave her a series of flickering glances, with wariness in her big brown eyes. It unnerved her. She forced herself to be nice to her, but a part of her knew that because of Gwendoline, she wanted nothing to do with a child, especially a girl. If she and Jack did marry, she would pack Marie Louise off to school.

It agitated her that a child of four seemed to glimpse her soul. Did Marie Louise know she was evil, in the way that small children and animals are said to know, and dislike, some bad people? *Don't be ridiculous*, Jane told herself.

At the picnic, Jane had become more impatient and angry with every minute. She wanted the girl gone, wanted to be away from her wary, even knowing, eyes, and was relieved when she got up and ran over to her nurse for a drink of lemonade, and they all went for a walk leaving her and Jack alone. Jack had started up to join them, and held his hand out to her to help her up, but she had asked him to stay because she needed to speak to him.

She had told him about Gwendoline because it seemed clear to her that Jack loved his child more than he loved her. And she'd wanted to punish him for it!

It had been a big mistake. Now he was adamant about finding his daughter! His paternal instinct surprised her, and for a child he never even knew.

It was all over with Jack Saint-Saens, because he had said so, unless she told him where she could find their daughter. Her protests that it would be impossible were in vain.

CHAPTER SIXTY

Two weeks after that, Mr. Saint-Saens had his long-awaited visit from Mr. Barrett-Smith.

He took delight in showing him all over the house and gardens that the visitor remembered from his holiday when the Ashtons lived there.

As they walked around the fish-ponds, Barrett-Smith complained that since he had arrived home to England, his father had done nothing except to burden him with work. He wished him to tour the entire estate, for he had a plan to improve it.

"So, I have been riding all over my land, seeing fields and hedges, inspecting streams and rivers, assessing cottages and villages and even towns. That, my friend, is the easy part. Unfortunately, many of the farmers have become involved with The Farmers Alliance and are demanding recompense for irrigations, machinery, and any modernising they have done on their houses and lands."

"If they have carried the expense, then perhaps they have a point."

"If they had requested permission to carry it out, my father would have refused it."

"But surely you would not wish them to continue their medieval farming methods, when better and more efficient ways have been developed?"

"I might think that way, Saint-Saens, but my father thinks otherwise. He is nearly seventy, you know. He has very fixed ideas about knowing one's place and thinks the Farmers Alliance is an invention of the devil. Father is old-fashioned about new methods and new ways of thinking. No matter how I might think, I have to carry out his wishes. I would not defy him."

"What is his plan?"

"He has studied the land clearances taking place elsewhere. Reclaiming the land for tillage and sheep grazing, instead of having numerous family farms.

It's very uneconomical, and of course sometimes the rents are very difficult to get out of them."

"In bad years?"

"Oh, and in good. There are always those tenants who are tardy with rent. Father would love to be free of rent-collecting."

"If you clear the farmers and cottagers off the land, what will they do?"

"My father knows quite a few men who have given their tenants compensation, money to go to America. But nothing has been decided yet."

"What if they do not want to move?"

"If Father decides to clear the lands, then they won't have a choice in the matter. But I say, Jack, I almost forgot to tell you—there is a very interesting section of our estate; there's nothing like it, I would say, in all of England. There's a river that flows down to the Thames, called the Wick, joining it very near the Estuary. It's a short, but wide tributary. And in the Wick, there is an island, sort of hidden away. It is inhabited, but my father has never visited it, nor can he remember if his father ever did. He has never heard of anybody going there. They're quite an independent people, about two or three hundred, nobody knows for sure. It is even said that they have their own King and have formulated their own Parliament! They live by fishing. But this is the most astonishing thing of all—nobody pays rent! They never have! Not a penny!"

"Extraordinary!" said Jack. "Do they have churches and schools?"

"A teacher got short shrift there one time. They have a building that functions as a church. But don't they sound quite savage? I wonder if they carry javelins and crossbows! I think I should be quite afraid to row over there without a suit of armour and an armed guard! Father has a history of the place in an ancient book in the library, written in Latin. It seems it was first inhabited by Roman soldiers who had married Englishwomen and didn't want to leave them behind when their legion was returning to Rome, so they took a boat, pretended they were going fishing, and wrecked it on the rocks. They got to Saltwick somehow and hid there for some time, and then brought their wives out. So it began. Nobody disturbed them or their descendants for many generations, and whether the present residents are all descended from these Romans, or others have joined them, is not known, but there are some dark-skinned people there, which is very intriguing indeed."

They walked on, leaving the fishponds for the stables.

"About the land clearances you spoke of—I hope you do not mind my stating my opinion. I think it would be quite unfair to push the farmers out, or to push cottagers off their little plots," said Jack quietly, feeding his favourite horse, Midnight, a few carrots he had carried with him.

"I would not like to do so—but if my father demands it, we shall proceed." was the reply. Jack did not know if Barrett-Smith was simply shifting the responsibility on his father to avoid debate, or whether he had genuine concerns for his tenants. "And as for that island in the Wick, we shall have to do something about *that*."

CHAPTER SIXTY-ONE

The small classroom was a motley collection of young people aged fourteen to eighteen. The big lads squeezed themselves behind the desks, and more than one wondered what they were doing there. But Mr. Saint-Saens was keen for them to learn to read and write, and they'd give it a shot. The skitted and larked about to cover their discomfort.

Gwen sat away from the boys, who she thought never looked at her anyway, because of her spectacles. The new scullery maid, Lucy, sat beside her. Gwen was proud to have been officially promoted to still room maid. Her pay increased to eleven pounds a year. Her duties were expanded, and she it was who had to serve the meals to the upper servants in Mrs. Higgins's room. The work was much easier—the constant drudgery of the scullery was largely behind her, though Mrs. Higgins was tremendously particular about cleanliness. She now got on famously with the housekeeper. Mrs. Higgins was the enthusiastic teacher of a willing pupil and Gwen's skills were improving every week,.

But at seventeen, was she too old to learn how to read and write properly?

The teacher arrived, and Gwen was very pleased when she saw him. It was Mr. Fleming. Everybody got to their feet with shuffling and banging noises. He wrote his name on the blackboard, led them in the Lord's Prayer and set one of the lads to distributing slates and chalk.

In the middle of the lesson, the door opened again, and Mr. Saint-Saens entered. All rose again.

"I wanted to see how you are all g

, and I quite miss it, but I'm not going to do Mr. Fleming here out of a situation."

He stayed a few minutes longer, and class resumed. After that, he often paid a visit, and Gwen wondered if he yearned to take over the class himself. He sometimes asked them questions or asked to see their writing. He bent to her by her desk and praised her handwriting, for she was a little ahead of the others. She looked up at him, seeing his face close for the first time, she saw his gentle expression—his eyes! She had never really seen them before, and it seemed that they were so like her own! A kind man like him would want to find his daughter and ensure that she was well provided for and happy! *Could it be her?* How she would love to be his daughter—but not that of Mrs. Westingham! No! She felt at ease with Mr. Saint-Saens. She still had not seen Mrs. Westingham, removing herself from every opportunity where they might perhaps meet. Not that she would be recognised, grown up and wearing spectacles. She rarely went upstairs, rarely beyond the housekeeper's rooms. If that woman was her mother, she dreaded meeting her and would never, ever reveal who she was, not even to gain a father, not even a good father like Mr. Saint-Saens. She had fleetingly wondered about getting another place but put it out of her head. She loved her still room work.

Some of the older lads dropped out after one or two classes, which disappointed Mr. Fleming, who warned the others that they had placed themselves at great disadvantage in the world by not persevering.

Gwen did not need any encouragement. She longed to unravel the mysteries of the books on the still room shelf, applied herself well and by the time the evenings were drawing in and the leaves were falling, she could make out the simple receipts in the books. Learning to read well showed her a new world. Mr. Fleming praised her. But even if he wasn't above her—there was one unsurmountable obstacle—he was not from Saltwick and would never understand how her heart was bound to the island.

One day, when Gwen was in the kitchen garden, Mr. Fleming happened to be going by the gate, so he came in and talked with her. He had a book with him.

"I was in Mr. Saint-Saens's library," he said, "and I chose this book for you. It's a book of poetry by George Herbert, a poet who lived a long time ago. See—this poem here—I want you to read that." He opened it at a marked page.

'I made a posie, while the day ran by.' Gwen's eye went to the next line. "Oh Mr. Fleming, it looks far too hard for me."

"Then do what you can, and I will help you during class with the parts you find difficult. I think you will like the imagery, though. How he uses pictures in his mind, in this case a posy of flowers, to express his own thoughts."

"Thank you, Mr. Fleming." Her eyes lingered with him as he went out the little gate.

Gwen slipped the book into her pocket. She hoped that Mrs. Higgins had not seen them.

Mr. Fleming proceeded to his lodgings, thinking. His pupil, Gwendoline Paul, was an interesting girl. He felt drawn to her in spite of himself, in spite of the differences in their rank. Nobody seemed to know much about her, except that she came from the Isle of Wight. Her hair, when he had been fortunate to glimpse it, was the colour of golden wheat. Her complexion was luminous. She moved with grace, but her servant's clothing was unbecoming. When he had met her unexpectedly one day by the river, he had secretly admired her figure clad in a flattering, but modest, blue gown. They had walked together for a little while, but she'd said little. Her spectacles made her shy, he thought. Most of his friends scorned girls with spectacles. Mr. Fleming thought they gave a girl an air of mystery, like a veil over her face, shielding her soul. He longed to see her eyes properly, he felt certain that much beauty was hidden there.

CHAPTER SIXTY-TWO

"**M**r. Jeremy Markham to see you, Madam." said Babs, with a little smirk.

"I don't know anybody of that name, but show him in." Jane settled herself down on a parlour chair by the fire. She hoped that this was not a man of any note—she had not bothered to do her hair today, and her dressing had been careless. Some days she felt that she did not care whether she lived or died; the chains, her constant companions, sapped her energy, and she would have put an end to it all long ago, were she not afraid of meeting God.

She looked with bewilderment as she recognised the visitor, who today was not wearing any livery, but an ordinary suit of clothes.

"It's you, Markham! I never thought—. What is this? Do you bear a message for me?"

"No, Madam. I do not, at least, not from Rockwell."

"What is this, then? Is there something amiss?"

"No, Madam. It's not like that at all. I want to be of assistance to you, Madam."

"Assistance to me! Are you applying for a position? There is none vacant. We are a very small household."

"Madam, that is not the kind of assistance I think you may need at this time. May I sit down?"

She indicated a chair, frowning at his smug familiarity.

"Tell me what it is about, Markham."

"It is a very delicate matter, Madam. I wish to return your mind to last summer, to the picnic at Holland Park. I could not but overhear a snippet of conversation between you and Mr. Saint-Saens, not through any wrongdoing on my part, but because I happened to be passing nearby, on my way to gather the plates."

"Go on," she said coldly.

"I understood that you may be set a very difficult task, in order to retain the friendship of my master."

Her expression darkened in embarrassment, then anger. She looked away briefly before saying:

"How dare you! Is your business blackmail, then? Will you spread my secret far and wide?"

"Not at all. Haven't I said I wish to assist you? Madam, it may not be impossible to satisfy Mr. Saint-Saens in this matter."

"Whatever do you mean, Markham?"

Jeremy Markham took a deep breath. His situation at Rockwell could depend on her reaction to what he was about to propose. He could be out on his ear by nightfall. But if worse came to worst, he had a bit saved, and his Uncle Jimmy, a butler to a great house in Devonshire, had promised him characters and to find him another position.

"I know of a girl, Mrs. Westingham."

There was a pause as he looked for her reaction.

"Go on." she said at last, as what he was saying began to sink in.

"I have an orphaned cousin, sixteen years old. She has fair hair, very handsome. She has grown up with my—and her—Uncle and Aunt Phillips in Newcastle-upon-Tyne."

"Go on," said Mrs. Westingham. She seemed to sit straighter and was more alert. "What does she look like?"

"I took the liberty of asking my uncle to send a likeness." Jeremy took a photograph from his pocket and handed it to Mrs. Westingham.

"She is comely. There's a delicacy about her features, how tall is she?"

"About your own height, Madam."

"Her eye-colour? It cannot be dark. We are both of us light-eyed."

"Very blue, Madam, like yours. Blue as forget-me-nots, and as charming as yours."

Mrs. Westingham gave him a sharp glance. He merely smiled.

"Does she know of this?"

"Yes, Madam. She knows and is game for it. It is a good opportunity for my cousin Elizabeth."

"In what line of business is your uncle, Markham?"

"He is a shopkeeper, Madam."

"A shopkeeper!" she burst out laughing. "You are jesting with me, are you not? You found out that my father was a shopkeeper?"

"No, Madam. Indeed I did not know that. I was not aware of that fact."

"It looks like this is meant to be, then. We shall have much to talk about shops, Miss Elizabeth and I, if this—but Markham—what do you intend to get out of it?"

"My principal aim is to be of service, Madam."

Mrs. Westingham's mouth twitched.

"You don't expect me to believe that."

"Having said that, Madam, I would like a remuneration of some kind."

"I must warn you that I do not have a lot of money, in fact, I am quite poor. But I can get something for you. How much do you have in mind?"

"Two hundred pounds, Madam."

"As much as that? You are very greedy."

"It takes one to know one, Madam."

He was impertinent, but could afford to be so.

"It will depend upon the success of the scheme, Markham. But I see we understand each other very well."

"You need have no fear of me, once everything is settled. I will leave the employ of Mr. Saint-Saens, Madam. With my remuneration I intend to get married, move to the North and start a business."

"Married! Who is your intended bride?"

"A Miss Paul, the still room maid at Rockwell."

"I'm sure I have never seen her, if she doesn't come upstairs."

"Shall I write to my uncle, Madam, and tell him that it is settled?"

"Yes, and I must decide what I shall say to Mr. Saint-Saens. How I came about information about Gwendoline. But what shall I do if he demands proof?"

"Do you not have any trusted friend who would say that she was the woman who arranged the adoption?"

"I could find somebody, I suppose." Mrs. Westingham saw more money disappearing in a bribe. She had few friends, but she knew plenty of people who would accept money to tell a lie. There had been one maidservant at Bullmere who had, for a half-sovereign into her palm, told many a fat lie for her to her late husband. She'd look Martha up.

"You can rely upon my discretion, Madam. As I will rely on yours, of course."

"Give me two weeks, then summon your cousin. In the meantime, I shall tell Mr. Saint-Saens that he may expect good news soon. I hope your cousin Elizabeth will be able to keep up the pretence, and she will have to be called—*Gwendoline*—and get used to that. She will have a very good life." As she spoke, Mrs. Westingham felt that old familiar feeling of distaste and guilt at mentioning her child's name. Her child who lay at the bottom of the river Wick. For the rest of her life she would have to pretend that this Elizabeth was her daughter and show her all the affection denied to the real Gwendoline. She was confident that the girl would play her part as best she could. Only a complete fool would throw away all that money, when a subterfuge meant it would keep her in luxury and ensure an advantageous marriage. She hoped that Jack would believe the story.

And having presented Elizabeth—*Gwendoline, Gwendoline!*—to Jack, she was certain that he would marry the mother of his long-lost daughter. That was a given.

She got up and held out her hand to Mr. Markham.

"Return to me this day two weeks," she said. "And we will make a definite plan then."

CHAPTER SIXTY-THREE

Mrs. Higgins was summoned once again to the study. She checked herself in the mirror before ascending the steps. She always did that now, and for the last several months she wore a bejewelled little pin in her frilled black satin cap, barely visible, but it sparkled when she passed a window.

She had frequent meetings with her employer, for his mother was increasingly forgetful, and though still in good physical health, she now required a nurse at night, and there were the nursery matters also to speak to him about. She often had to ask him about new clothes and shoes for the rapidly growing girl, and for anything that was required that was beyond the daily budget.

He motioned her to be seated. The study was in much better order since Mr. Fleming had arrived, and she looked about it with approval.

Mr. Saint-Saens was smiling. He made a steeple of his forefingers as he rested his hands on the desk.

"Mrs. Higgins, Mrs. Higgins," he began in a gentle, amused reproach. "I have heard that you don't allow followers downstairs."

"I do not, sir! And the maids—they are all very chaste. That I know. Not one of them will get into trouble before they are married."

"But how are the maids to find their husbands, Mrs. Higgins?"

"Oh." She was a little taken aback, before recovering herself. "They might choose to remain single, as I am. The unmarried life is not so bad, you know. I, for one, am—happy enough in this state." She looked away and seemed to tilt her chin just the tiniest bit. The September sunlight coming in the window caught the little amethyst in her cap and it sparkled.

He smiled gently but composed himself before her eyes returned to his face.

"There is a lovelorn member of our staff, Mrs.

Higgins, who wishes to court a maid, but is in trepidation in case the maid may be dismissed."

"I am no tyrant!" she said with a little indignation. "Whoever he is, I am sure I would be very understanding. I have the maids' welfare at heart, you know."

"Of course, you have, and of course you are not a tyrant, Mrs. Higgins," he soothed her. "I would not tolerate tyranny in my house. But he does not wish to break the rules."

"I think I know the couple to whom you refer, Mr. Saint-Saens. She is a good girl, I have no fears for her, and I'm sure he is honourable, if a little forward, if I may say so, taking the long hallway out of the house, in order to chat to whomever he meets. I've had occasion to rattle my keys!"

"I only know the maid slightly from the schoolroom, Mrs. Higgins. A modest, self-effacing girl, very keen to read well, the sighing lover tells me. He has been teaching her poetry, a sure way to fall in love. I can vouch for his honour. Now I beg you, will you drop your prejudice against courtship and marriage?"

"I was never prejudiced, sir. And I will alter the rule, as you wish," she said, after an indignant pause. Without knowing it, she again patted the brooch upon her bosom, today a large amethyst set in silver filigree to match her cap.

"I am very happy to hear it," he said.

After she departed, his mood altered to the other matter never far from his mind since the day at Holland Park. His lost daughter. What had become of the child? And why had Jane not told him before now? He was in a difficult situation. He wanted to find Gwendoline, but if she perchance came to live with him, honour would demand that he marry her mother! Was this her scheme? And how would he ever be sure that the girl presented, if she was found, was his daughter? It seemed impossible. He had a wild idea to call Mrs. Higgins again to confide in her. She was a sensible, intelligent woman, and not without feelings. She sometimes allowed her mask to fall a little, to reveal a woman who would love to be loved. It would be unkind to confide his personal dilemma to her, to involve her.

What a shame that Johnson was such a crusty old bachelor!

CHAPTER SIXTY-FOUR

"I have found the woman who took our child," Jane Westingham said to Jack the next time they met. It was a wet October day and they were in the carriage, on their way to an Art Gallery. "I have visited her, and she told me that she still has the address of the couple who adopted her."

He asked her many questions about the woman Martha James, and she fielded them as best she could.

They reached the Gallery and arm in arm entered the large ornate hall with marble floors and staid pillars. Art bored Jane but she accompanied Jack because she knew it pleased him. Also, one could meet important people in an Art Gallery.

"There are three artists exhibiting; Frederic Leighton, William Holman Hunt and Benjamin Waites," said Jack, consulting the pamphlet. "Mr. Waites is just to our left, so we might as well see his collection first." He led her into a small, quiet room leading off the hall, where a few guests strolled by rows of land and seascapes.

"Good afternoon," said a bearded man, who bowed and introduced himself as the artist.

"You are fond of Nature, sir." Jack said, looking about. "You favour watercolours, yes? As I like them myself, I imagine we will have a very pleasant time here."

"Yes, but please do not go away without seeing my Saltwick Collection, it is in another room just off this one, and though I may say so myself, it was as much as work of love as of art, on my part."

"Saltwick, you say? What is that?"

"Ah! Nobody knows of Saltwick! It is a funny little island in a tributary of the Thames Estuary. It's inhabited by fishermen and basket-weavers who are rather jealous of their privacy and their own way of life. A reclusive people. Instead of landscapes, I found inspiration in its inhabitants. If you like, we could view them now, for there is a story attached to nearly every face, and I have a little time just now to tell you of them. The portrait means so much more when you know something about the person."

"I believe it is the very island that Barrett-Smith told me of! Let's see them first then, shall we?"

They entered another room off the main one, filled with portraits mounted in frames on walls of pale blue.

"An ugly looking people!" Jane said, looking about. "What did you see in them, Mr. Waites? Look at that man's weather-beaten face."

"That, Madam, is the King of Saltwick. I see a great deal of life in his face."

"The King! How droll! And here—?"

"His wife."

"Her wrinkles put me in mind of a cobweb. She's spent her life under the sun. So brown! Are you sure this is England, Mr. Waites, and not Spain?" She left Jack's side to get closer. She was in good spirits, finding something ridiculous in the portraits.

"Jane, come look at this." Jack said suddenly from across the room. "There's something quite beautiful about this one. If you admire beauty, you will love this."

But Jane was not listening. "Some of these people are dark foreigners, Mr. Waites. And here's a doctor! A doctor! Wild-looking man! He couldn't possibly be a real doctor. A witch-doctor perhaps."

Mr. Waites had deserted the unappreciative visitor to join Mr. Saint-Saens.

"Ah, you have found my favourite, sir! I painted this one ten—no, twelve years ago. 1863 I think. She was a very interesting subject. The natives told me that she was not from the island. And there is a most extraordinary story attached to this child!"

Jane joined them at last, and Mr. Waites addressed her.

"The islanders told me that they took her from the River Wick, almost dead, after an attempt at murder *by her own mother*. Can you imagine, Madam? I see your woman's heart is greatly affected. Her name is Gwendoline, so I named it *'Gwendoline's Grief'*. Look at her eyes, Madam. I pray you, did you ever see such sadness? Look at her eyes. Do they not ask a question? The question *Why*?"

Jane looked straight into the sight she dreaded the

most—the blue-green eyes of her daughter Gwendoline looking straight at her. She drew back in terror and fell to the floor. Her limbs jerked in violent seizures. The cries that came from her seemed to come from the pit of hell.

CHAPTER SIXTY-FIVE

Jane Westingham's screams were heard throughout the Gallery and even outside on the street. A policeman was called, then a doctor. A crowd gathered. The coachman and footmen were located, and Jack, Markham and Coach got her to the carriage and bore her away to her home, where Jack stayed for a time, the doctor in attendance upon her, while Babs and another maid put her to bed.

Her seizures had ceased, and her body was calm. But she appeared to neither hear nor see. She was awake and staring at the ceiling when Jack entered her room but was insensible to everything and everybody.

Jack was in agonies. Why had she—what was it that

—was that their Gwendoline and did she—his mind refused to put the unthinkable question that lurked before him. He paced back and forth in her chamber, stopping to stare at her at intervals, and his heart rejected what his head was telling him. Even if he could have put the question to her, she could not speak to respond. She had not uttered a word since the screams abated.

He went to her and shook her by the shoulders, but she did not respond, though her eyes were staring and terrified. Her lips began to move as if she was speaking rapidly to herself. She seemed to be in a private Hell.

"I must know!" he cried to her. "I must! This is our Gwendoline, is it not? Is it not?" He shook her again, but he could get no good from her, and let her be. He crammed his hat on his head and went home.

CHAPTER SIXTY-SIX

It was all over the Servants' Hall that Mrs. Westingham had thrown a seizure and had to be carried home. Mrs. Higgins heard of it and forbade anybody to speak of it. It was none of their business, she said. If they wanted to help in any way, gossip would not do it. Private prayer for the parties concerned would help.

Jeremy Markham went about his duties optimistic that she would recover. Women had a habit of throwing hysterics and had to be slapped out of them. He hoped that the doctor had, by now, cured her. He wouldn't have any of that nonsense with Gwen.

It was time to tell Gwen his plans. He found his way to the still room the following day and saw her reading. She pushed the book hastily into her pocket at his approach.

"I thought you were Mrs. Higgins," she said, taking it out again. "I was sure I heard a jangle."

"She's down the hallway. What's that?"

"Poetry."

Markham took the book out of her hands.

"I don't want you readin' too much, Gwen."

"Whyever not?"

"Where did you get it, anyway?"

"From Mr. Fleming."

"I've seen 'im sneakin' around the gardens at the back. Was it you he was seeing?"

"He doesn't sneak, and yes, it was me."

"I don't like this, Gwen!"

"You don't like what?"

"If I see 'im, I'll knock 'im down. He's up to no good."

"Don't be ridiculous, and give me back my book!"

"I'm surprised at you. Gwen." He pocketed the book and left the still room.

"Come back," she hissed after him, after checking that Mrs. Higgins was nowhere to be seen. "That book belongs to the library here!"

Markham turned smartly and walked up to her. He threw the book at her feet.

"If you ever see him again, I won't marry you."

Gwen stared at him.

"I don't remember you asking me, Markham, and if you do, I'll say no," she snapped.

"C'mon Gwen, you know we're going to get married."

Gwen heard the jangle of keys.

"I've never encouraged you, Markham. I don't like how you sneak about. Now go away."

"You are a tease, Gwen. I know we're going to be married and go North." He caught her wrist.

"You're dreaming, Markham! Get it out of your head! Let me go! You don't love me, and I don't love you, and I'm going home as soon as I've learned my trade, and I'm going to work for myself."

"Nobody else is going to want to marry you, Gwen, with your glimmers." He was furious, and went off as the jangling got nearer. Shaking with anger, Gwen began to scrub the table. What presumption! How rude—and cruel! Her eyes misted and she couldn't see for a few moments. Thankfully, Mrs. Higgins passed the door without coming in.

She would have to leave Rockwell.

CHAPTER SIXTY-SEVEN

G wen need not have worried about Mrs. Higgins that day. The housekeeper had just received an urgent summons to go to her sitting room. What could be amiss? Was Mrs. Brown's nurse there, or Perkins her maid? Was there something wrong with Marie Louise?

Mr. Saint-Saens was standing about in her sitting-room, his brow streaked with anxious worry.

"Mrs, Higgins, please excuse me for coming to your rooms. But I need to speak with you most urgently, and privately, and my mother is in the drawing room and Mr. Fleming is engaged in some work in my study."

"Please make yourself comfortable, sir. I shall ring for tea directly."

It was Gwen's duty to answer the housekeeper's bell and she was greatly surprised to find her with Mr. Saint-Saens. He sat with an air of dejection, his head lowered, his hands clasped.

She sped downstairs, made a pot of tea, set a tray and brought it up, just in time to hear, "she will have to be watched constantly and cannot be left alone. Everything she says must be noted, most especially if she mentions the name *'Gwendoline.'* Mrs. Westingham may be guilty of a heinous crime when the child was but six years old."

Mrs. Higgins cast him a warning glance, so he said nothing more.

Holding her breath and biting her lip, she set the tray down on the table. If the cups clattered nervously in their saucers, they did not notice.

"Thank you, Gwen." said Mrs. Higgins quietly as she rushed away.

"Gwen? A Gwen here? Of course, that's the girl who is learning to read. Where is this Gwen from?" asked Mr. Saint-Saens as Mrs. Higgins handed him a cup of tea.

"The Isle of Wight, I believe."

"It's a common enough name, *Gwendoline*," he said. "I'm losing hope, Mrs. Higgins. Or—if I may be so bold—can I call you Leonore? You seem to be more like a friend to me, than anybody else in the world, if the truth be told."

"Of course, sir. You may call me Leonore." Mrs. Higgins heart leaped.

He asked her to engage nurses to be in constant attendance upon Mrs. Westingham, and she understood that his quest was to find out as much as he could about his missing daughter—the daughter he suspected she tried to murder when she was six years old. They were to report every word she said, if she spoke.

CHAPTER SIXTY-EIGHT

Gwen hardly knew where she was going, her heart was so full of emotion. She ran out the tradesmen's entrance down to the bank of the Thames and sat on a bench in a little recessed area partly hidden by trees and bushes. She could be alone here. She pulled her shawl about her, for the late afternoon was chilly.

Mrs. Westingham may be guilty of a heinous crime.

Now she was certain.

"Hey!" she heard a voice. Jeremy Markham! What was he doing here? He flopped down beside her.

"I see you regret it already. I might forgive you, if you are sorry. Give me a kiss. We're engaged."

"No!" she turned from him, but he flung his arms about her in a tight grip.

"I've waited too long," he said. "C'mon, just a kiss then."

"Let me go!"

"Let her go!" Mr. Fleming appeared in her view, and grasped Markham by the collar, throwing him off the bench. Markham was much taller than he, and rose with his fists ready for a fight, but William ducked and slammed him to the grass. He held him by his front collar.

"Get away from her; never touch her again." He let him go. Markham struggled to his feet and hurried away.

She was seated on the bench, crying, digging her knuckles into her eyes. He lowered himself to sit beside her and reached out his hand to touch hers.

"Don't do that. You'll hurt your eyes. Look, here's my handkerchief."

In the fracas, her spectacles had come off. Her hands away from her eyes, she took the handkerchief and gently dabbed them.

"Thank you," she said, then looked at him. He seemed mesmerised.

"What beautiful eyes," he said, "hid behind those lenses! I hope you don't mind my giving you a compliment," he added hastily.

"I don't mind. I'm so lucky you were passing by," she said.

"I wasn't. I saw you leave the house and there seemed to be some agitation in your haste. Then I saw him follow. I wondered—I mean—I did not know if there was a mutual attachment there, but if he meant any evil, I was going to put a stop to it. You were running away from him, were you not?"

"I was not running from 'im, but from a very difficult situation I find myself in." this was followed by fresh tears. "He just saw me and followed, but not to 'elp me, only to harass me to marry him. He knows nothing of this trouble I have. Nor would he care, if he knew. I am glad to be rid of 'im." She shivered and pulled her shawl even closer about her.

William wished he could put his arms about her, but she might mistake his intention. So he just said, "Is your trouble very bad, or am I prying?"

"It seems impossible to resolve, because I'm sure I'm

related to somebody, and if the other person comes to live here, and I'm related to her as well—if what I suspect is true—I do not want to be under the same roof as Mrs. Westingham, if Mr. Saint-Saens brings her to Rockwell to be nursed!"

"Good grief. Why do you not begin at the beginning, Miss Paul."

"That's the beginning, Mr. Fleming. My name isn't Paul."

CHAPTER SIXTY-NINE

They returned to the house hand in hand. Fleming reassured her that the 'follower rule' was gone. It did not matter anyway; her father's closeness to Mrs. Westingham frightened her, but before she left, she would tell him that she was almost sure that she was his daughter, and to protect Marie Louise, she would have to tell him the truth.

Gwen was half-afraid to go to Mr. Saint-Saens's study, and almost lost heart halfway up the stairs, but William pushed her gently forward. He knocked at the dreaded door, and at the 'come in!' was admitted.

Mr. Saint-Saens was surprised to see her. William

placed his hand on the small of her back in a gentle nudge for her to go forward to him. Gwen glanced at him briefly for support, and he winked, before she looked at the very bewildered Mr. Saint-Saens again and said, "Mr. Saint-Saens, sir—I'm Gwendoline Compton, and I'm from Saltwick Island."

He rose as if in a dream and came around the desk, gazing at her intently.

"Compton! There is no way you could have known that name, is there?"

"I was born Compton, sir, and lived with my Aunt Ellen for six years, then she—my mother—took me and tried—to drown me at Rush Pier, in the river Wick."

Ellen. Jane had a sister Ellen. And if this was a ploy from Jane, if she had set this girl up, she would certainly not have told her to say she had made an attempt upon her life!

He probed gently, without seeming to interrogate, and remembering the portrait, asked her if any people came to the island, in summer?

"Artists, sir."

"To paint what? Landscapes?"

"Some of them painted landscapes, yes."

"Did any paint portraits?"

"Oh yes, an artist came and took my portrait when I was a child. He made me sit for it outside our house. He said he was going to exhibit it. He was Mr. Waites. He often came to the island to paint us."

"I have seen that portrait, Gwendoline. It was that very portrait that caused Mrs. Westingham's collapse. She recognised you."

He gently took her hands and kissed her forehead. She could not be false. If he had any doubts left, he could compare her memories with those of Mr. Waites.

Gwen tears flowed. Her Papa! Her real Papa!

William Fleming made as if to go, but a look from Gwen made him stay. She felt frightened of this turn of events in her life, she did not know what to do next, and William gave her courage.

She went downstairs again after a time—Mrs. Higgins was not in the house, and it was she who would see to her changed environment, and she decided to carry on as normal. Unfortunately, the first person she met was Markham. He had been waiting for her.

"I'm sorry, Gwen. Awfully sorry. Look here, I know you prefer him to me. All's fair in love and war. It's just that I was going to come into money, and I thought we could make a life together, you and me. I shall leave anyway."

"I think that's a good idea." Gwen said. She remembered suddenly that it was Markham's snooping that had led to her knowing who she really was, and her attitude softened.

"We shall part as friends." she said.

"I'm coming into money," he whispered. His apologies over, he was his bragging self again. "I have to wait, though, for a while, until Mrs. Westingham's better."

"Mrs. Westingham? What have you got to do with my mother?" It slipped out.

Markham paled, looked askance at her, and withdrew. He gave notice that evening.

By then, a very astonished Mrs. Higgins had, after another urgent summons from her employer, moved Gwendoline to one of the best rooms upstairs. Mr. Saint-Saens had to explain it all to his mother, who forgot it as soon as she was told. Gwen dined in the housekeeper's room that evening. It was the wisest way, for now, for Downstairs had got hold of the information, and she had a horror of the dining room, and of being waited upon by Markham, of all people.

Gwen tried not to think about her mother.

CHAPTER SEVENTY

S ALTWICK ISLAND

The doctor had just emerged from the post office in Rush when a man accosted him outside.

"Doctor Gibson." The man touched his hat.

"To whom do I have the pleasure—?"

"My name is George Harold. I am steward to Mr. Barrett-Smith."

"Mr. Barrett-Smith." Dr. Gibson knew who Barrett-Smith was, and he had the suspicion that no good was to come from this encounter. The islanders knew nothing of Barrett-Smith but Gibson, who read the newspapers, knew.

"Yes. I'm sure you know he owns all the land hereabouts, including Saltwick Island."

Gibson waited.

"He wishes me to visit the Island, and I plan to go today," continued Mr. Harold.

"Very well." Dr. Gibson made to go, but Mr. Harold raised his hand to stop him.

"If you will excuse me, I would beg for five minutes of your time. Perhaps we could go over there—" he indicated a beerhouse.

"I do not have very long, Mr. Harold. My boatman's wife is very near her time, and he and I want to hasten back. He is waiting at the pier."

"I understand. I won't keep you long."

Together the two men entered the Seagull's Nest, where they settled in a quiet corner.

"Mr. Barrett-Smith is in need of information, and thinks it would be best if this information is known before I go to the Island."

Dr. Gibson gave a wry smile. The police had advised them of this approach, he was sure. Mr. Harold produced a notebook and pencil. Dr. Gibson frowned. He began to feel that if he were spotted, he'd be branded a traitor. And he was King!

"I am ready, sir." He said calmly, taking a sip of bitter.

"How many households on the island?"

"I have no idea."

"How many residences? You don't know?"

"No, I don't. Why should I know? I never counted them."

"What is the population, roughly?"

"I don't know. It fluctuates. People come and go, wherever there's work."

Mr. Harold's eyes were becoming a little impatient.

"One hundred? Two? Four? A thousand?"

"Perhaps two hundred."

"So, there might be about fifty households, if there are four persons per household?"

"I suppose that may be the case. If the Government had come to take a census, which they never did, you'd have that information."

The population had dwindled in recent years, more

young people had left, and others had admitted themselves to the workhouse. Last winter had seen off several of the old people.

The doctor took out his watch.

"I will come to the point then, Doctor, since you want to be off. Mr. Barrett-Smith has an offer to make you. You may live on the mainland, a forty-shilling freeholder, with a right to vote in elections, if you will be responsible for collecting rents on Saltwick."

"Rents on Saltwick! Are you out of your mind, sir? The people of Saltwick can barely feed themselves! Fish stocks are low since that new factory opened, and the vegetables are rotting in the fields! Now, you tell me that they have to pay rent? Do you want them all to die?"

"There's no necessity for that," rapped Mr. Harold. "I'm sure you're aware of the alternative, should Mr. Barrett-Smith meet resistance on this matter."

"What would that be?"

"Eviction, sir."

Dr. Gibson was silent. Then he asked, "How much rent will every family have to pay?"

"That will be assessed upon inspection of the house and plots of land."

"There are no houses. There are wretched cabins and cottages. I myself live in a cottage. And there is very little currency upon the island. Most of my patients pay me in kind."

"I believe there is a King of Saltwick." said Mr. Harold, half-amused, half-contemptuous.

"And you think he must live in a palace. There is no King as in Royalty as we understand it. That's a myth put about by the people here. You will tell me next there is a Parliament."

"Is there not?"

"No. We are British, Mr. Harold. We place British stamps upon our letters. I have to leave you now. May I ask how you plan to go to Saltwick? Who will row you there?"

There was silence.

"Ah. A police boat. Of course." Dr. Gibson swept away.

CHAPTER SEVENTY-ONE

D
r. Gibson's boat was soon overtaken by the faster, steam-powered police boat, the first time that Dr. Gibson had seen one in use. There would be no time to alert the populace about what was about to happen. His boatman, John McDonnell, rowed as fast as he could. He was worried about Betty. He also muttered that he hoped his father had time to hide the still.

"I'm afraid, lad, that discovery of the still will be the least of Saltwick's worries soon."

The steward did not need the men to be present to assess the land and the houses. He and a surveyor moved from cabin to cottage to cabin, writing in their notebooks and making drawings. By the time Dr. Gibson came puffing up the hill, they were a quarter-way through. The police, six in all, strolled about. There was little for them to do, except issue a stern warning to Mrs. Marcus who jabbed at Mr. Harold with a knitting needle while she was telling him to get off her land.

The women were angry and rushed to the doctor as soon as they saw him.

"Who are these men? Why are the police here? Can't you do something?"

"It's the World," he replied. "It's come to us. We can't stop it."

Perhaps a policeman mentioned it to one of the women, or perhaps something was overheard, but it was soon known that they would be compelled to pay rents. At that, John McDonnell hot-footed it to the caves, and soon a ragged army of Saltwick men, armed with sticks and knives, marched along the twisting road from the cliffs. At the sight of them, the police formed a line and drew their batons.

"Allow me to talk with them," requested the doctor. The inspector agreed.

The hasty Council meeting took place in a sunken area by the road, a spot where there was once a house, or a courtyard, but now so completely overgrown that only an archaeological dig could reveal what it had been. The men, soon joined by the women, sat down and the doctor told them what had happened that morning. A few of the older men, led by the ousted Mr. Marcus, tried to incite feeling against the doctor, thinking that he had led the Police there, and that he was in the pay of this Smith-Barrett-or Barrett-Smith, whoever the scoundrel was. But they were shouted down by the younger element. Dr. Gibson, with great difficulty, made it clear to the meeting that there was no way to win this war. Everything was ranged against them. They were British, and this was the law of Britain.

In the middle of it all, Betty McDonnell laboured in her cabin and the doctor was called away to attend her. The cry of the new-born baby was heard by two policemen some hours later.

"I wonder if that'll be the last child to be born here," the young recruit said to the other. "But I 'ope we don't have to evict these people. I din't join the force for that. They're not criminals."

"You've never done an eviction, then? The first few are 'ard with the women and children crying, then you get used to it."

CHAPTER SEVENTY-TWO

CHELSEA

Gwen woke up the first morning in her elegant room and drew back the curtains. There was a clear view of the river. She reflected that it was not at all as nice as the view she had had from her little cabin on Saltwick, and once again she longed to go back there. Would her father allow her to go? If not, she would just run away. She quietly reflected that while she liked her father, and could love him, she had no idea what living with him would be like, and she would fly away like a bird if he was strict with her. She knew how to earn her living.

She dressed and sent a bemused Mabel away, saying she had always looked after herself. Her father understood the reluctance and told Mrs. Higgins to be patient. One did not learn to be rich overnight. It was Mrs. Higgins who told her how she should conduct herself for the remainder of the morning after breakfast, she could walk about the house freely, but would be expected to spend most of her morning with her grandmother, the other woman of the house.

"We should get in touch with Mrs. Westingham's sister." Mrs. Higgins said, speaking in her father's study. "Gwen, if you remember the address, we shall write a letter."

"And the Westinghams should know also." said her father. "I will find them."

"You are not happy, Gwen, what's the matter?" asked Mrs. Higgins.

"I'm not happy even to hear her name," Gwen replied. "I still have memories of that day. Am I a bad person, to hate her?"

"We shall talk of it later, Gwen. Go to your grandmother now."

Mr. Saint-Saens thought that Mrs. Higgins was an admirable teacher for his eldest daughter, who would need wise guidance in her new life. She had told him in a little burst of impatience that it was impossible for her to begin to call Gwen *Miss*. She had far too much on her mind and could not remember it. And Gwen did not expect it. He had said that it was quite all right. She was in all ways but one, mistress of the house …

All ways but one … Leonore told herself sternly not to take anything from his remark.

Mrs. Brown thought she was Abigail, her granddaughter from Robert, on a visit, and Gwen played along as best she could, although she darted upstairs to her father to please teach her the names of her aunt, uncle, and cousins, bursting in on him and an amused William, who wrote the names and approximate ages for her as her father called them out, and then made her read them to him.

She glided after that, agreeing with everything her grandmother said. Yes, Gerald was a little terror. And Margaret sang like a nightingale. Aunt Penelope was in very good health. And Uncle Thomas, yes, he was healthy too.

"No, I just remembered." said Mrs. Brown, looking up from a tapestry fire screen she was working upon. "Did Thomas not die last year? His horse threw him!"

"Oh, I am sorry, Grandmother. I thought you said —*Horace.*"

"Horace? Who is he? There is no Horace."

"There is a very good friend of Papa's named Horace, and we call him Uncle."

"And he is in good health, is he?"

"Very much so, Grandmamma."

She tried to speak better, all she had to do was to try to speak like Mrs. Higgins, who spoke well, but she felt that she was a character in a play.

Mrs. Brown took a nap after luncheon and the parties convened in the drawing room to find out what was to be done with Mrs. Westingham. William was present, as was Mrs. Higgins. Gwen was the first to speak.

"Mr. Saint-Saens—Father—I don't want the police. I don't want her to hang. But I don't want to hear her name or see her." As she spoke, she knew that she did not hate her mother. Was there another feeling that was not hatred but was grievous sorrow— betrayal perhaps? She had a fleeting image of Jesus in Gethsemane. He must have felt the pain of betrayal, but He did not hate his betrayer.

"Nobody is going to call the police," her father said. "She would not hang by the way, because you lived."

Gwen was not happy with this either. How could she enjoy her life, when her own mother, wicked as she was, was suffering daily in a prison? Was there no outcome where she, Gwen, could be made happy? Why was her heart in turmoil with this? All her life, for almost as long as she could remember, she'd been a girl whose mother tried to kill her. Sometimes it shocked her anew.

William leaned over and pressed her hand. She looked at him gratefully. He winked at her and her heart lightened.

"At present, she isn't in a fit state to face a judge," her father said. "Leonore, did you contact Mrs. Peake?"

Everybody startled at the use of Mrs. Higgins's Christian name. Gwen found herself astonished that she had one. Wait till she saw Madge and Peggy! It dismayed her that all that easy friendship and banter with her friends was over. She'd love to hear what they had to say about *Leonore*.

"I have urged her to come." Mrs. Higgins looked steadily at Jack. It seemed to the remaining two in the room that Jack's glance lingered with her.

CHAPTER SEVENTY-THREE

That night Gwen awoke suddenly. A wisp of a dream vanished before she could remember it, but it had something to do with her mother. She became aware of a hope—a craving—to find out if her mother was sorry. Why would it mean anything to her? She realised that she felt a desperate wish to be loved by her. Mrs. Paul she regarded as her mother—but this other woman, in whose womb she had grown, who had given her life—she wanted to be loved by her also. She had the extraordinary impulse, born from she knew not where, to see her mother again. She fell asleep again and this time, she awoke having dreamt vividly of Auntie Nuru and a story she had told her once.

She gave herself over to a full expression of her heartbreak. She cried for the rest of the night. Anger, sadness, grief, resentment and hope churned in her heart. She battled her thoughts, she prayed, she fought with herself, she fought with God. Something was being asked of her. Finally, she fell asleep, exhausted. When she awoke, a golden October sun was streaming in, and she had slept late.

CHAPTER SEVENTY-FOUR

J ane was aware of people about her bed. Why had they come? She deserved nothing. Not Ellen pressing her hand. Not Walter, whose father she had neglected, kissing her forehead, telling her he was praying for her. They must not have set him against her, then. Not Jack, whose eyes were downcast and face was sorrowful. Certainly not the young woman with Jack's eyes, *Gwendoline*. A beautiful young woman, a girl she ought to be proud of.

Hell existed and she had been there for the past several days. A fire of torment burned in her mind and she had no ability to distract herself. She was physically powerless, and mentally she was fastened by the chains she had made for herself.

She hated herself, not others. They were good people. She was not. What a wasted life. After she closed her eyes for the last time, her Hell would continue, forever. This was a foretaste of Eternity.

Now they all left the room, except Gwendoline. After the initial distress of seeing her portrait, it was a relief to her that Gwen was alive. Had she known that she would never know a happy day after her crime, she would never have done it. Gwen was a fine young woman. She took after Jack.

"Mother," she heard Gwendoline say. "I want you to know that I'm trying to forgive you. It's difficult, but I'm going to keep at it. I realise I love you. Because you're my mother and because God loves you. He will forgive you if you're sorry for everything. He will! Mamma, if you are sorry for what you tried to do to me, and if you can hear and understand me, please repent. You're a lost sheep, Mamma. Jesus is still looking for you. He has never given up! Allow him to find you, please! Papa has called a clergyman and he will give you the Last Rites—the decision is yours."

Jane not only heard but for the first time in her life, she felt touched by someone's love for her, love she did not deserve. Gwen's words went deeper than anything her own mother had ever said in her worshipful praise of her; any clumsy, harsh word her father had tried to admonish her with; even any romantic words Jack, Daniel, or any of her lovers had uttered. She was deeply affected.

Her only thought now was to repent deeply and allow herself to be found by God. She'd been lost most of her life. How dreadful she could not convey to Gwendoline that she appreciated her words! Gwen left the room, and the clergyman entered.

CHAPTER SEVENTY-FIVE

Gwendoline almost wished she had never mentioned *Horace*. Mrs. Brown could not forget this mythical friend of Robert's, and was rather offended that her son had never introduced him. Gwendoline kept her company in the drawing room for part of every day; and the rest of the day she was in her beloved still room; or with Marie Louise, either in the nursery or outdoors, which both preferred. She read poetry, guided by William. She liked poems about Nature best, and the Psalms that described God's power in Nature. William had an unending supply of verses. His merry eyes cheered her, and she treasured his care for her happiness and well-being.

Gwen kept herself very busy. Her mind was at peace about her mother, now dead three months. She had done what she could. It was almost Christmas. In the spring, she was going back to Saltwick. Perhaps not to live there, she concluded. But she wanted to see everybody. What had become of her old house? She would ask her father to take her to Saltwick Island and introduce him to the people who had been her dear friends in her younger years. She hoped that William would come as well.

On Christmas Eve, Mrs. Higgins found a little wrapped box in her room. It contained a diamond brooch and came with a note.

"From Jack, with love. If you feel for me as I do for you, please sit with us at dinner tonight, and wear this."

It was the happiest day of Leonore's life. She donned her best gown, a black lace shawl and the diamond brooch, but the sparkles from the diamonds were nothing compared to those in her eyes.

William and Gwen walked happily in the grounds every day and along by the river. She expected a declaration, but none was forthcoming. Perhaps he felt he had not enough money to marry, yet. But she was sure she had his heart, and he had told her that he loved her.

Her father went away on business in January for three weeks. When he returned, there was a very happy event in Christchurch, the wedding of Mr. Saint-Saens to Mrs. Higgins. Gwen was bridesmaid and met the rest of her family, Robert and her cousins, and a large celebration was held in Rockwell.

"He will declare himself now," thought Gwendoline, after she had danced almost every dance with William. Instead, when they went out on the balcony, and he took her hands and told her that he had something to tell her—but his words were not those that she wished to hear.

CHAPTER SEVENTY-SIX

SALTWICK ISLAND

A party of tourists were rowed to Saltwick Island on a bright but cold Monday morning in late March. They were Mr. and Mrs. Saint-Saens and their daughters Gwendoline and Marie Louise.

Gwen was excited, and only one cloud shadowed her life. William had left his situation to take up a new position elsewhere. It was a bitter blow. He told her he loved her and promised to write, but no letter had come. At least, not yet. Her father and new mother—Mrs. Saint-Saens had ordered her to call her *Mother* or *Mamma*—had told her she was being impatient, and she had made herself busy getting ready for the trip to Saltwick.

They hired a boat and a boatman from Rush. As the old sights came into Gwen's view and grew larger and larger, she became eager and happy. The beach, the mudflats—she told Mrs. Saint-Saens that she must allow her to take Marie Louise to walk barefoot in the mud. The herons called in the rushes, and the gulls swooped. A wind was blowing, and she savoured its freshness. The purple and orange spring tablecloth was upon the hillside, as if to welcome her anew.

But she could not see any sign of life upon the island —no children ran down to the shore as they usually did when a boat was seen to be arriving.

Where was everybody?

Soon they were walking up the beach. Gwendoline pointed out every familiar sight. Up the slope they went, Marie Louise wanting that very moment to take off her boots and to be taken to the mud.

The hamlets came into view. Still there was silence. They came upon the old Paul cabin, standing where it had always stood, the rock still outside the door.

"Somebody has whitewashed the cabin," she said, pleased. "Look! A new roof! Perhaps there's someone living here, Papa. Look, here's the rock where I sat for the painting. Oh, the Whites' house is still there too, and well it looks!"

She pushed in the door of her cabin. Nobody knocked on Saltwick Island.

"Halloo! Is there somebody here? There has to be, for the fire is burning. The table is laid for a meal! New red curtains! I like them! But no bundles of withies in the loft, and no baskets at all!"

"Is that you, Gwen?" called a woman's voice from the front door. Gwen wheeled around. An old woman was there, and a young woman with a baby in her arms.

"Mrs. White! Betty! Is it you?"

"Yes, I'm McDonnell now! Oh, you are looking well! Meet young John here." Betty held out her smiling baby.

"Betty, oh what a bonny little child! Do you live here, then?"

"No, I live in the McDonnell's. Mamma still lives in her house, though."

"It does my heart good to see you back, Gwennie," said Mrs. White, embracing her.

"Where are all the children? Nobody ran down to meet the boat!"

"Why, they are all in school! There's a new school. And Dr. Gibson has a proper dispensary ..."

"Changes!" cried Gwen. "Oh no—but I'm glad to hear of the school! And the dispensary—"

"Some changes are good I suppose. Your father insisted on them." said Mrs White, with a half-resigned glance at Mr. Saint-Saens.

"Who?"

"Mr. Saint-Saens there! Is not that your father?"

"Papa! What's happening?"

They walked up the winding path. It was very quiet until a ship's horn sounded in the distance. Its familiar blast made her smile with happiness. But what had her father to tell her?

"I bought the island from a man named Barrett-Smith. Last November, I wrote to him about Saltwick Island because I knew it was so dear to you. He wrote back and said that his father was about to evict everybody and pull down the cottages. I made an offer immediately. I have no interest in owning land, Gwen, for my own profit. The families are all freeholders with no rent to pay, but they've had to make alterations in their way of life. But here's the school—let's go in."

It was a new, whitewashed building, long and low. They could hear the children chanting their tables.

"Papa, the teacher will hardly like it if we simply walk in."

"I don't think he'll mind at all. Come on."

The door opened into the classroom and the first person she saw, at the top of the room, was William Fleming. He raised his arm in a big wave, gave the children a half-day there and then and joined them amidst their whoops of joy as they tumbled out to enjoy their freedom.

Gwen felt that she was in a dream. William took her hand and kissed it. "Surprise, isn't it? Blame your father. He would not allow me to tell you!"

They fell behind the others. In between her expressions of surprised happiness of being with William again, Gwen greeted joyfully everybody she saw, gathering news of this person and that, and she garnered snippets of the trying times they had had in the intervening years. Mr. Beasley and Old Man Foster were dead, and Bob White had married a

Northern girl and wrote often from Yorkshire. Many other young people had gone away. They'd had a visit from their MP who had promised them a great deal of benefits, which few understood and fewer believed, for their opinion of the World seemed to be unchanged.

Seeing her animated interest in everybody and everything, William asked her:

"Would you like to live in Saltwick again, Gwen?"

"I know I would! Do—do you like it here, William?"

"I loved it from the first. So *far from the madding crowd,*' as Thomas Hardy would put it. You haven't met him yet; that's another treat in store. We *will* have a library here someday."

"Oh! Is that a post-office? And a little shop too? That's the room where the whiskey-still was! Is it gone?"

"Yes, and a good thing too. The police found it and carried it off, but no charges were brought—your father's influence. Your father also had a talk with Barrett-Smith and the MP about the textile factory ruining the fish, so fishing is coming back, but the stocks will not be good for some years, and the locals will have to attract tourists to live."

"I never knew anything was amiss," Gwen said wonderingly.

"Your father will tell you about it all. But Gwen— enough for now—there is a question I wish to ask you."

She knew what it was, and led him away from the main party, and they ran together to the spot she liked best, the hillside where they had for company the purple avens and orange marigolds. There, with a sudden happy breeze blowing her hat off and her hair loosened in the wind, she said 'Yes' and William took her in his arms and they kissed, and another ship's horn blasted in the distance as if in celebration.

The newly engaged couple rejoined the family a little later on, and returned to the schoolmaster's house, the very one that Gwen had grown up in, to eat a lunch of fresh bread, grilled sole and boiled potatoes prepared by Mrs. White and Betty, and they raised mugs of strong hot tea to toast the couple. After that, they doffed their boots and took Marie Louise to walk in the mud, for she had been very patient.

Thank you so much for reading. We hope you really

enjoyed the story. Please consider leaving a positive review on Amazon if you did.

WOULD YOU LIKE FREE BOOKS EVERY WEEK FROM PUREREAD?

Click Here and sign up to receive PureRead updates so we can send them to you each and every week.

Much love, and thanks again,

Your Friends at PureRead

Printed in Great Britain
by Amazon